'Do you remember that first night, Colby? *Really* remember it, I mean?'

'I can still recall the taste of your mouth, Liz, the feel of your skin, your soft breasts against my bare chest. Oh, I remember it. Like it happened last night...'

She swallowed hard and looked away. 'I guess you do.'

'It was a special night,' he said, touching her cheek, pulling her closer to his body. 'We had a special relationship.'

Liz knew what she wanted—what they both wanted. She tested her courage as she tried to balance desire against pride, strength against weakness, the past against the future.

'I want that night again, Colby,' she whispered. 'I know it's selfish and it's wrong. But I want you to make love to me one more time...'

D1324604

Dear Reader,

In everyone's life there are certain moments that are special—events that change the course of a person's destiny. For me, February 14, 1984, was memorable because that is the day Ronn proposed. We were in front of a fireplace, sharing a glass of champagne... and I'll leave the rest to your imagination.

Valentine's Day is also special for Liz and Colby in *Change of Heart*. Liz was born on Valentine's Day, and married Colby on her eighteenth birthday. But youth and poverty and parents worked against them, and they split. Now, ten years later, they meet on Valentine's Day once more. Sparks fly, memories of love fill their hearts, and over a glass of champagne they decide to see if the magic is still there...

My hope is that this Valentine's Day will be as lovely and memorable for you as it was for Liz and Colby, and for my husband and myself.

Best wishes,

Janice Kaiser

CHANGE OF HEART

BY

JANICE KAISER

MILLS & BOON®

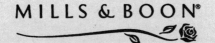

MILLS & BOON and MILLS & BOON with the Rose Device are registered trademarks of the publisher. TEMPTATION is a registered trademark of Harlequin Enterprises Limited, used under licence.

First published in Great Britain 1998 by Harlequin Mills & Boon Limited, Eton House, 18-24 Paradise Road, Richmond, Surrey TW9 1SR

© Belles Lettres, Inc. 1997

ISBN 0 263 80806 8

For Edris and David
A Love Until the End of Time

21-9802

Printed and bound in Great Britain by Caledonian International Book Manufacturing Ltd, Glasgow

February 13

THE EYES OF EVERY WOMAN in the room were staring at him.

"Would you look at those buns," Angela whispered. "What a bod." Her tone was more wistful than lustful. "The last guy I went out with was built like a fire hydrant. The one before that like a scarecrow. Why can't I snag an Adonis just once?" She sighed.

Wendy leaned toward her, watching the young man over the rim of her champagne flute. "Quit it," she muttered. "I don't need to be reminded."

"Of what?" Angela chided. "That for the second Valentine's Day in a row you'll be going to bed with Jay Leno?"

"Shut up and eat a chocolate," Wendy groused, pointing to the enormous heart-shaped box of candy in the middle of the table.

Liz Cabot had been listening to her friends bantering. And she couldn't help smiling, though with nearly as much sadness as amusement. This was, after all, her last meeting of the Thursday Night Club For Divorcées, Spinsters and Other Reprobates. But in spite of the fact that this evening was, for her at least, filled with mixed emotions, her friends were doing their bawdy best to keep her spirits up.

The evening's conversation had tended to center around their usual favorite topics: men and sex. But then, with the waiter they had tonight, it would have been hard to keep their minds on anything else. The man was gorgeous. A real hunk. So good-looking, he was almost pretty. And though Liz normally wasn't attracted to a man solely because of his looks, she'd been admiring him right along with everyone else.

Angela and Wendy elbowed each other as the group collectively watched the waiter hoist a tray of dirty dishes to his shoulder. The room was silent as he made his way toward the door, muscles rippling under the little white jacket that was cropped at the waist. He had the slim hips of a matador and, yes, Liz had to concur, great buns.

"Oh, waiter!" Wendy's voice rang out over the hush.

The young man with the pale eyes and olive skin stopped and looked back at the table.

"Another bottle of champagne! Put it on a separate tab."

The waiter nodded. "Yes, ma'am." Everyone seemed to exhale at once as he left the private dining room that had been decorated with red crêpe-paper streamers, sequined hearts and balloons.

Moira, Liz's best friend, shook her head. "I'm embarrassed for all of us," she said. "We're acting like schoolgirls."

"That looks like drool running down *your* chin," Ariel Stephens said dryly, her long fingers wrapped elegantly around her wineglass. "Or are you going to claim it's the chocolates?"

They all laughed, even Pam Wilson, though this was her very first meeting of the Thursday Night Club. Liz had been watching the earnest little brunette, wondering if anyone with such rosy-cheeked innocence would fit in. "They can be cruel," Liz had told her before the meeting.

The Thursday Night Club tended to get a bit ribald—and Lord knew, Liz herself had been more than a bit priggish at first. But in time she had learned to let her hair down on Thursdays. "It's easier to act like a lady six days a week if you refrain from all pretense of propriety for a least one," was the way Wendy justified it.

The club had been meeting at the Clairbourne, a small but exclusive midtown businessman's hotel, for three years—ever since Jane Martin was head of marketing for the place. Ultimately Jane had left the group when she married and moved away from New York, but the "Thursday night girls" kept coming to the Clairbourne because the management continued to give them a good deal.

"I can fantasize as well as the next person," Moira replied to Ariel. "I just wonder if we need to collectively undress him. Somehow, it doesn't seem very dignified. Even for us."

"I think Moira's going soft," Angela said.

"She's just feeling sentimental," Wendy intoned. "She *is* the last of the original Mohicans, you know."

It was true that Liz's departure would make Moira the sole surviving charter member. The club's other two had already gone on to marital bliss, Liz being the most recent of the founders to "sell out."

Moira had masked her sadness about Liz's departure with chiding remarks. "I expect to die an emeritus member," Moira had said wistfully when she first saw Liz's ring. "Let's face it, I'm the only true-blue spinster in the group. I should have known you didn't have the guts for it—not for the long haul."

Liz had hugged her, but they both knew it was the passing of an era. To prevent extinction, though, the founders had made provision for the possibility of defections. The original four members had added two more, then approved a rule that no one ever left the club without finding a replacement. Pam was Liz's.

Rules for membership in the Thursday Night Club were strict. To join, a woman had to be aggressively single, not just between men. Of course, they all recognized that it wasn't easy to avoid temptation. Life, as Wendy had often said, offered opportunities to succumb to the "weakness of the flesh." But once you had a ring on your finger you had a month to come to your senses before you were expelled. This was the night they would ceremoniously boot Liz out.

"Being the last of the founders is a distinction I wear proudly," Moira said to Wendy. "Somebody's got to be loyal to the group."

"Yeah, sure," Ariel said. "And when Mr. Wonderful leads you off by the hand you'll be crying crocodile tears for the rest of us suckers, same as Liz is for you."

Liz and Moira exchanged looks, and Liz reached over and took her friend's hand. Moira's eyes glistened. "Last nights" for a departing member were always emotional. And Liz knew this would be extra hard on Moira because the two of them had been so very close. Not that they wouldn't be seeing each other, of course, but they both knew it wouldn't be the same.

"Back to Mr. Tight Buns...." Angela said.

Ariel rolled her eyes. "Girl, do you have a one-track mind, or what?"

"No. Well, maybe I do. But either way, I've got a serious question," she said, sounding very serious indeed. "We all agree our waiter *looks* fabulous. He might be dumb as a stump and have no sense of humor, but let's assume for the sake of argument that he's great in the sack. Is there anyone here who wouldn't take him home tonight?"

"You mean for a one-night stand?" Wendy said. "Anonymous sex?"

"Yeah."

"Fantasizing is one thing," Moira said, "but if you mean actually doing it..."

Everyone maintained a decorous silence.

"Okay, let me rephrase the question," Angela said. "Is there anyone brave enough to admit she's had sex with a stranger? Some guy you didn't know but who had all the right moves."

The women exchanged looks.

"No comment," Ariel said after a moment or two.

They all laughed.

Ariel arched an expressive brow, trying hard to affect an aloof demeanor, though a smile was about to break out. She'd been a fashion model, but when it became apparent she'd never make it big, she had switched to management. Now she headed up one of New York's largest agencies. Ariel, with her wide brown eyes and smooth cocoa skin, was gorgeous.

"There's anonymous and there's anonymous," she said. "It depends on how anonymous you mean."

"I think we can talk a good game," Liz said with a laugh. "But when it comes right down to it, nobody would really do it."

"It would be stupid," Moira added.

"In a way that's sad," Angela lamented. "Not that I advocate promiscuity for the sake of promiscuity, but don't you think everyone should have an experience like that just once?''

"I'd have to be pretty damned drunk even to think about it, let alone do it," Moira said. "Besides, I don't think I'd enjoy it. Not if I didn't know the guy. Call me a prude."

"You're a prude," Ariel said.

More laughter.

Moira McKenzie was an analyst for a brokerage firm on Wall Street. She was almost six feet tall and had bright natural red hair. Liz, who couldn't have loved her more, was physically her opposite. She was small and blond and, as her dad had liked to say, scrappy. Until she'd gone to law school, she'd considered it a quality more useful to a wrestler than a woman. Around her feisty friends in the Thursday Night Club, though, she tended to be relatively reserved, if only because being outrageous was the group's dominant characteristic.

Liz, who'd been feeling sentimental all day, had to struggle to get into a ribald mood. Yet Angela's question about anonymous sex had piqued her curiosity. "Angela, why do you think it's so sad?" she asked. "Men are the ones who seem to revel in one-night stands, but I don't think that's true of women. I'm not saying that we should be virgins when we marry, but what can a woman really get from anonymous sex?"

"The same thing as a man," Wendy interjected. "Excitement. Living out a fantasy."

"Sounds dangerous to me," Pam said. She'd said very little since she'd arrived and everybody looked at her.

Angela Cavioli, an accountant by day, and "a wild and crazy woman" by night, as she liked to say, put a sisterly hand on Pam's shoulder. "Life is dangerous, sweetie."

"Yes, but why take unnecessary chances?"

"We're talking about the allure, the excitement of living on the edge," Wendy said. "Not that anybody would want to do it all the time, of course, but why not once?" She stuck her tongue in her cheek. "Or in Ariel's case, two or three or four times."

"Keep going, girlfriend," Ariel deadpanned.

"Right on!" Angela enthused. They all knew Ariel loved being outrageous and played it up.

"So, you'd really like to have a one-night stand with somebody you didn't know?" Moira asked.

Wendy reflected for a moment, taking the question seriously. "I agree with Angela. Maybe it's something every girl ought to do once. Probably just before she marries...so that it's out of the way and she can say she's done it."

"Like a rite of passage," Angela said, twisting her empty champagne glass between her fingers.

"Not a bad idea," Ariel said. "Maybe we should make it a club tradition. On a girl's last night, we buy her a man. How's that sound, Liz?"

Though not one to blush easily, Liz did color. "Ever so kind," she said, "but I think I'll pass."

"It wouldn't be disloyal to Grayson...not if you didn't know the guy," Angela chimed in.

"No," Wendy added, "you'd be doing him a favor by getting other men out of your system. Once you've lived your fantasy, you could settle down to be the nice little housewife he wants."

"That's not what Grayson wants," Liz said defensively.

"Well, he certainly doesn't want you chasing other

men," Wendy replied. "Which is why you should live out your fantasies now, while you're free. Think of all the women sitting across from their middle-aged husbands at the breakfast table wondering what would have happened if they'd climbed on the back of that motorcycle the time the guy with long hair and rippling muscles asked them to."

"Thanks," Liz said over the laughter, "but I've already lived out my motorcycle fantasy."

There was a stunned silence.

"You rode off with a strange guy on a motorcycle?" Angela asked.

"Not exactly. But close."

"Listen to this, ladies," Ariel said, "the girl's been holding out on us. Her last night and she reveals she has a past!"

Liz had to laugh. Colby Sommers was a good deal more than "a past." For better or worse, he'd been the major fantasy man in her life! Even that might be an understatement.

She glanced at Pam, who seemed a little overwhelmed. Like Liz, Pam was a lawyer, a new associate in the same firm, Krantz, Markham & Warren.

"If you aren't going to launch a new club tradition, Liz," Wendy said, "the least you can do is tell us the story."

"But I've told it before. Moira knows all about it."

"Yes, but that was before our time."

"Come on, give!" they said, egging her on.

Just then the door opened and the waiter entered. The group took a collective breath as he approached.

Liz had to admit he had a certain something. Watching him as he removed the cork from the champagne, combined with all the talk about sexual fantasies, had gotten her to thinking about her own wants and needs.

At a certain level, the notion of a night of wild unbridled sex with a perfect stranger—provided, of course, she'd never see him again—had a certain appeal. But what troubled her was that she could so easily envision it. An engaged woman should be so deeply in love that other men simply didn't exist. At least that was Liz's theory. So what was wrong with her?

Grayson Bartholomew, the man who was to be her husband, was ideal. Both being lawyers, they had much in common and, both being lawyers, as their friends had said in jest, they deserved each other. Liz's mother phrased it best when she said, "Who but a lawyer could put up with you, dear?"

Not that she was all that bad, but Liz had grit. She wasn't afraid to assert herself. And it took a tolerant, patient, self-confident man to appreciate her type. Dear Grayson, she reminded herself, was all of those things. And yet in spite of that, here she was, feeling guilty as hell because she didn't have the kind of passion for him she thought she ought to have.

Liz absently watched the waiter circle the table, pouring champagne. Fascinated though she was, she knew her uneasiness had nothing to do with him. It was something crying out from within, something she didn't fully understand.

When the waiter leaned over her shoulder, pouring wine into her glass, she could feel the warmth of his body and she smelled his masculine scent. A twinge went through her. Liz saw that same feeling was reflected in Angela's eyes, and Wendy's sardonic smile. It wasn't mere lust. What was she feeling? The power of her own feminine sexuality? Maybe that was it. Maybe she didn't want to let go of her freedom.

She'd wondered about that all day. At first, she'd assumed her feeling of uneasiness had been because this would be her last meeting of the Thursday Night Club. But there was something else bothering her. That letter she'd received a few days ago—the one from Colby Sommers—had been playing on her mind. In fact, it was probably a big part of the problem.

She'd tried not to think about it. Colby had been her major romantic fantasy, true, but he was also an unpleasant reminder of some things she'd much rather forget. That was how life worked. Everything had its price.

The waiter poured the last of the champagne into Pam's glass and stepped back. "Care for anything else, ladies?" he asked politely.

Somebody tittered. Moira shifted uncomfortably. Liz hoped nobody would say anything suggestive. But Wendy spoke, stopping the waiter before he could leave.

"I have a question," Wendy said to the man.

Liz and Moira groaned in unison. That was both the beauty and the horror of the Thursday Night Club— you could never be sure what crazy thing might happen. When Jane Martin had gotten engaged to Toby Haugen, the women rented Playboy Bunny costumes and crashed his bachelor party. That adventure had been Wendy's idea. She was an executive with a Madison Avenue advertising firm. Surprise was her watchword.

The waiter looked expectant.

"She isn't going to say something to embarrass me,

is she?" Liz said to Moira out of the corner of her mouth.

"Somehow, I think so."

"Hypothetically," Wendy said in her most business-like tone, "how much money would it take for you to jump out of a cake with nothing on but a G-string?"

Angela began to giggle. Pam turned beet red, and Liz could do nothing but roll her eyes.

The waiter broke into a smile. "Actually, I used to do that, miss. Before I married. They paid me two-fifty. The agency got the rest. But if you're asking if I do it now, I can't. My wife wouldn't like it. Besides, I have baby daughters. Twins."

"Twin girls. How nice," Wendy said weakly.

Everyone fell silent. There was general embarrassment. Liz was ready to die, but then so was most everyone else.

"But if you ladies want," the waiter said earnestly, "I know someone who—"

"No," Moira said, interjecting, "that's not necessary. It was just a hypothetical question."

The man frowned. "What do you mean?"

"It was a joke," Liz said, hoping to smooth things over. "Just a joke."

"Oh, I see," he replied, grinning.

Liz gave a sigh of relief when he turned for the door. It wasn't until then that she realized how much she'd changed. She no longer fit into the group. Grayson had made more of an impact on her life than she'd thought. Yet ironically, something about that didn't feel comfortable. Was it because it was all so new, and she hadn't adjusted to the prospect of marriage?

After the waiter had gone, Ariel turned to Wendy. "Your karma sucks."

"He was married," Wendy groaned. "How was I supposed to know?"

"What the hell, at least we've got more champagne," Angela enthused. "With good wine, we don't need a naked man."

"Funny, I always thought wine and naked men went together," Ariel said dryly.

"You would."

Ariel's eyes flashed. But before she could say anything, Moira, who'd always been the club's peacemaker, quickly got to her feet.

"I propose we drink to Liz," she said. "After all, this is her farewell meeting." Turning to her, she went on. "You've been my best friend for years, so it's hard watching you go. I'll still be seeing you, of course...."

"Yeah, at baby showers," Angela piped up, bringing a laugh.

"But Thursday nights won't be the same. We'll miss you."

"Hear, hear!"

They all drank.

Liz was touched. "Thanks. I'm going to miss you guys, too."

"We have one other little piece of business to attend to," Moira said. "Tomorrow is not only Valentine's Day, it's our departing sister's birthday."

There was another hooray.

"Happy birthday, Liz!" Moira cried over the din.

They lifted their glasses and drank together. There were more cheers. Liz's eyes teared up. She was surprised at how sentimental she felt.

"Let's do the cards," Wendy enthused. "I found the world's meanest and I'm dying for everybody to see it."

They dug birthday cards out of their purses and Liz did the ceremonial "reading." The club had an agreement that there'd be no presents, but the member who gave the best card got a minibox of truffles from the birthday girl. Pam won by a unanimous vote. Her card was truly filthy.

"How can someone who looks so sweet be so bad?" Angela asked when Liz presented Pam with the box of truffles.

"She's a shark by profession," Wendy groused. "I think it's time we reconsider our rules of admission. No more lawyers!"

They discussed that, then Angela said, "Am I the only one to admit that tonight will probably be the high point of Valentine's Day?"

"Ugh," Wendy said. "Black Friday. Mine's looking bleak at the moment, sorry to say. Anybody got a date tomorrow besides Liz?"

"I do," Ariel volunteered.

"You always do," Angela said. "You could get dates with guys if you never left the ladies' room. Anybody else?"

"A group of us from the office are going out," Pam said.

"Group dates don't count," Wendy said. "Moira?"

"Valentine's Day at home...and alone."

"So maybe being engaged is good for something, after all," Angela said. "You've always got a date for Valentine's Day."

Everybody hissed. Wendy almost choked on her wine.

"Be honest, Liz," Ariel said. "Doesn't a part of you wonder if it isn't a mistake to give all this up for a man?"

Liz smiled weakly. Ariel couldn't have known how close to home that question was. But, of course, Liz wasn't about to open up a can of worms by discussing it—especially when she didn't understand it herself.

"Hey, wait a minute, girl," Ariel said. "Weren't you about to tell us about your one-night stand when the daddy of the twins interrupted?"

"Yeah!" several others added. "Let's hear about it."

Liz was sorry now that she'd said anything. "It wasn't a one-night stand," she replied. "It was sort of living out a fantasy...."

"Well, share," Ariel said. "Tell us the good parts."

"Yeah," Angela said, "we haven't had a war story tonight."

"And this is your last chance as a member," Wendy chimed in.

Liz and Moira exchanged wistful looks. It had been a tradition that at each meeting at least one juicy story was told. Some were happy stories—a sexy weekend skiing in Vermont with the office heartthrob. Others were horror stories—a date from hell with the guy in the apartment across the hall. Liz had told her share, but it had been a while since she'd talked about Colby Sommers—before all the members but Moira had joined the club.

"I'm not sure you want to hear about my former husband," Liz said.

"You were married, girlfriend?" Ariel said, her big dark eyes opening wide. "I didn't know that."

"For about fifteen minutes. When I was a kid. My parents got it annulled, so I guess I'm technically not even a divorcée."

"Hey, who cares?" Angela said, taking a gulp of

champagne. "As long as there's a good fantasy involved."

"It seemed good at the time, but after ten years I've lost perspective. The only reason it came to mind is because I got a letter from Colby a couple of days ago."

"You did?" Moira said, surprised.

"No big deal. He wrote to me about a business proposition. He's coming to New York next week. To discuss the sale of some property we jointly own."

"Good ol' Colby's coming to New York, huh?" Moira said, flipping back her red curls and smiling knowingly. "I don't believe it."

"How old were you?" Angela asked.

"Eighteen."

"My God, you were a child."

"Where's he from, anyway?" Wendy asked.

"Texas."

"Liz was married to a cowboy," Moira explained. "Not a costume cowboy, an honest-to-goodness one."

"My gawd," Wendy droned. "I didn't know real people married cowboys. I thought only cowgirls did."

"Honey," Ariel said to Liz, holding her champagne glass with haughty elegance, "this sounds like a story you'd better start at the beginning."

"You really want to hear?"

"Better than hearing about Wendy's trip to Club Med...for the third time."

Wendy made a hissing sound at Ariel.

"It's a Valentine's Day story," Moira said.

"Is it ever," Liz said, groaning. "Half the major events in my life seem to fall on Valentine's Day."

"So tell us about your cowboy," Angela said, scooting to the edge of her chair.

Liz took a long drink, wondering if she really

wanted to do this. Colby Sommers, she'd come to realize, hadn't faded from memory quite as thoroughly as
she'd previously thought. In fact, over the past few
days, he'd seemed to have risen from the ash heap of
memory like the mythical phoenix.

"What happened doesn't make much sense," Liz began, "unless you know my background. Mother's from
an old Connecticut family. Dad was a Texan. They met
during the Vietnam War and the romance lasted just
long enough for me to be born. As soon as my father
got back from Nam, things fell apart. After a year of the
ranch and Texas, Mom divorced and brought me home
to Connecticut.

"I only saw my dad a few times growing up. But
when I graduated from high school, Dad sent me a
ticket so I could visit him, saying he wanted to know
me better. I wasn't getting along with Mother then, so,
to spite her, I went to Texas."

"Let me guess," Wendy said. "Your ex was the irresistible hired hand."

"Just about. Colby was Dad's godson. His parents
had died during his sophomore year at Texas A&M. To
support himself he got a job with an oil company and
lived on Dad's ranch. He was twenty-three, and a gorgeous hunk. The first time I saw him, my knees started
shaking and my mouth sagged open."

There was a cheer.

"As soon as he smiled at me, I knew I was a dead
duck."

Hoots and hurrahs.

"I'm embarrassed just thinking about it," she said.

"Tell us all the juicy details," Angela insisted. "How
long before he...ah...snagged you?"

"He kissed me the first time we were alone together.

But I waited two weeks before sneaking out to the bunkhouse where he slept. I went back several times after that. It was a month before Dad caught us. Colby swore he intended to marry me. Being with him seemed so good, I was thrilled by the notion."

"So what happened?"

"Dad wanted to discuss it with Mother. Needless to say, she came unglued and grabbed the next plane south. This was the day before Valentine's Day, when I'd be old enough to marry without parental consent."

"So did you elope?" Angela asked.

"When my father drove to San Antonio to meet Mother at the airport, Colby and I took off. We were married by a justice of the peace. I was in sneakers and jeans; Colby in his hat and boots."

"On Valentine's Day," Pam said. "Nice touch."

"Right. Real romantic," Liz said with a laugh. "We were so scared, we forgot to kiss. When the judge called me Mrs. Sommers, I broke into tears."

"That's really sweet," Pam said.

It had been a while since Liz had thought of that. She'd been frightened, but also desperately happy. Even now she could not think of Colby without feeling bittersweet. He had been so good for her, and yet so very wrong for her. So irresistible, and yet so alien from the kind of guys she'd known.

"What happened?" Wendy asked.

"We went to New Orleans. Colby had eight hundred and forty bucks. We got a room in a hotel that rented by the week near the French Quarter. Colby drove a delivery truck. I waited tables. We were so poor we couldn't even afford to go to a movie. When we had a spare buck, we'd take the St. Charles Avenue trolley out to Audubon Park and visit the zoo or toss a Frisbee.

"On Sundays I'd make Colby put on a coat and tie and take me to the antique shops on Royal Street in the Quarter and we'd pick out the gorgeous stuff we'd buy when we were rich. But it was a lost cause. When our money ran out, Colby said we'd have to go back to Texas because he could make a living wage in the oil business.

"Those days in New Orleans were the happiest and saddest of my life. I was too young and stupid to know better, but I lived each day like it was my last. We made love incessantly because for some reason we thought we wanted a baby. We talked about it, I think in an attempt to feel we had a normal life. But I didn't have the courage to stop taking the Pill, thank God.

"But we both knew that going back to Texas meant giving up. As soon as we got to Dad's ranch, he all but locked me up until Mother and my stepfather Weldon could take me back home. I screamed to high heaven, but in my heart I knew Colby and I no more belonged together than my mother and father did.

"Colby didn't give up, though. He drove his battered old pickup to Connecticut to get me. We had an emotional reunion, but the handwriting was already on the wall. My mother knew it was up to her to give me the necessary backbone. In the end, I agreed to an annulment. That fall I enrolled at Columbia. Four years later I went to law school, never looking back. I haven't seen Colby Sommers since."

There was a silence. Liz stared at a red balloon bobbing and weaving in front of a heating duct in the corner, remembering the Valentine's Day card, the balloons and the single red rose Colby had gotten her the night of their wedding. He'd bought the balloons at a mom-and-pop grocery store. He had found the rose in someone's yard and cut it off the bush with his pocket-knife.

Her eyes glistened at the recollection. She could picture Colby blowing up the balloons as she opened her Valentine's Day card. It had been one of those little cards schoolchildren give each other, but it was all they'd had at the store.

To this day, she remembered wakening in the middle of the night and smelling the rose, which she'd put in a water glass on the bedstand. She'd lain there in the dark, listening to Colby's soft snoring, the bud against her nose. The next day she'd held it in her hand, sniffing it as they drove to New Orleans. Later, she'd pressed the bud in a Bible. She still had the rose somewhere—probably in a keepsake box in her closet at home.

"So, has your ex remarried?" Pam asked.

Liz shrugged. "I have no idea."

"What sort of business does he have with you?" Moira asked.

"When Dad died, he left his ranch to us jointly. My father considered him as much his child as he did me."

"Then you own a big spread in Texas!" Wendy said gleefully.

Liz laughed. "Hardly. I think when he died there was only seventy-five acres, though he'd had much more at one time. It's not worth much, but according to Colby's letter they've found oil in the area, and he wants to exploit what he can. I have no idea what the mineral rights on seventy-five acres are worth, but it can't be much."

"Then why's he coming all the way to New York to do the deal?" Moira asked. "Couldn't it be handled by mail?"

"I don't know his reasoning."

"Maybe he's curious what you're like, now that you're a big girl," Angela said, sipping her champagne.

"And tomorrow would be your tenth anniversary," Moira added. "Maybe Angela's right. Maybe Colby's sentimental and that's why he's coming."

"He did have a sentimental side," Liz admitted, "but I don't think that's it. He's made no attempt to see me before, so the only reason he's coming now has to be because he considers this property settlement to be important."

They fell into a contemplative silence.

"How are we going to find out what happens, if this is your last meeting?" Angela asked.

Liz chuckled. "Moira can let you know."

Everyone had finished their champagne. Wendy looked at her watch. "Anybody for going over to First Avenue and hitting a few clubs? Who knows, your Valentine's Day date may be waiting on a bar stool, dejected and lonely."

"I'll go," Angela enthused.

"Count me in," Ariel added.

They looked at Pam. She shrugged, her rosy cheeks turning red. "Why not?"

All eyes turned to Moira and Liz.

"Last chance for a rowdy night of merrymaking, Liz."

"Tempted as I am, no," she said with a laugh. "But thanks."

"Moira?"

"I think I'll see the matron home," Moira said.

"Dirty work, but somebody's got to do it," Wendy quipped. "Come on, girls, get out your wallets."

They settled the bill and everyone put on their coats. There were hugs all around before the four others left, giddy with laughter. Liz and Moira lingered.

"Hope this wasn't too hard on you," Moira said.

Liz shook her head. "We gave Jane and Lily a bad time when they broke ranks. I was one of the worst."

"It's all in fun."

"But I remember being a bit jealous, deep down," Liz said. "I'm sad to think that's how all of you feel."

"We're happy for you, and you know it."

They left their private room and went down the hall. The laughter of their friends echoed down the stairs from the hotel lobby. They exchanged smiles.

"So, you and Grayson have big plans for tomorrow night?"

"No," Liz replied. "He offered to take me out, but who needs the crowds? I'm making a nice quiet dinner at my place."

"Sounds romantic. I'd change places with you in a minute."

Liz put her arm around Moira's waist and gave her a squeeze.

They came to the stairs and started up to the lobby.

"You want to hear something funny," Liz said. "I'm not as happy now that the engagement is official as I expected to be."

"Really?"

"It's odd, but it almost seems anticlimactic."

"Maybe you're nervous about getting married."

"Moira, I'm not nervous. If anything, I feel guilty."

"That's quite an admission."

They came to the top of the stairs and stopped.

"I was impulsive the first time around," Liz said. "So this time I opted for cool, collected and rational.

It's what I want, but somehow it doesn't feel right. Am I crazy, or what?"

"I think you're gun-shy, Liz. Under that tough veneer, you're a cream puff."

Liz laughed. "You know me too well, kiddo."

"You said it yourself—Valentine's Day has always been pivotal for you."

"Well, I'm praying for a nice quiet one this time."

They peered across the lobby. Their friends had already gone outside. Moira suggested they wait until the others had gotten taxis before going out to find their own. It was snowing and cold and neither of them were eager to leave the warm lobby.

They watched their friends clowning as they tried to get a cab. Wendy ventured into the middle of the street before getting splashed by a passing truck. Liz and Moira had to chuckle.

"Are we already starting to seem like a bunch of silly schoolgirls to you?" Moira asked.

"Naw, I'll love you even when I'm old and gray and have ten grandchildren."

"Wendy will be the same fifty years from now," Moira said as they watched their friend brushing slush off her coat, "still chasing down taxis with her cane, I'm sure."

"And talking nostalgically about Club Med."

They both laughed.

A taxi pulled up out front just then and the Thursday Night girls got excited, obviously pleased by their good fortune. They stepped back as the rear door opened.

A tall lanky man in a sheepskin coat, jeans and holding a cowboy hat got out. Wendy and Angela checked him out and Ariel gave him one of her model poses. Moira, watching, chuckled.

"Speaking of cowboys."

The man put on his Stetson and gave the women a smile as he grabbed his bag and stepped back to watch them pile into the cab. Liz stared with eerie fascination, her mind questioning, even as she assured herself it couldn't be. But when he turned and the light from inside the hotel struck his face, she was able to see his characteristic grin. Her heart stopped.

"Oh my God."

Moira looked at her. "What's the matter?"

"That guy out there, Moira...it's Colby Sommers."

2

COLBY SOMMERS CHUCKLED when the tall, black beauty waved at him through the steamy window of the taxi. He watched, smiling to himself, as the cab lurched back into traffic. *City girls*, he thought, shaking his head. Here one moment, gone the next. But, of course, this faster way of living had its advantages.

As the taxi headed up the street, Colby glanced at the dark sky. Soft snowflakes drifted down like delicate parachutes onto the urban landscape. Their purity was in stark contrast to the harsh streets, the steel-and-concrete wasteland awash in slush.

Nor was it like the winter-bleak plateau and snowy buttes he'd left behind in Texas—the open, endless, yawning silence by day, and the purr or growl of the wind by night. In the back country, days could pass without an indication of the existence of another soul, save the occasional crack of a hunting rifle in some distant canyon, or the jagged scar of a vapor trail stretching across the azure sky.

He cherished the vast emptiness of west Texas, the solitude, but he liked his fun, too. That was what made these trips to New York—or Dallas or New Orleans—such a pleasure. Colby was a man of contrasting tastes. And he had a healthy respect for women who could appreciate that.

Taking a last, deep breath of wintery air, he turned

to the entrance of the hotel and went inside. Coming through the second set of doors, he saw two more sweet city women—a tall redhead with hair poking from beneath her fur-trimmed hat, and a smaller blonde whose curls cascaded from under a soft black beret. The blonde was the prettier of the two, causing him to give her a second glance as he strode by.

Their eyes met briefly, then he was past her. Something about the woman seemed familiar, though it was as much the way she regarded him as her actual appearance. As his mind tried to sort it out, he stopped, turning on his heels. The blonde and her companion were just going out the door when it hit him.

"Lizzy?" he called out, unsure.

She stopped, her hand on the door. The other woman, the redhead, glanced back first, her expression wary. But then the little one turned around, too. There was consternation in her eyes, but he instantly saw that it was her.

"Lizzy, it *is* you."

"Hello...Colby," she said, sounding reluctant to acknowledge him by name.

"Good Lord," he said, incredulous.

His eyes scanned her. She was bundled up in a heavy coat. It was difficult to get an impression of her, but the trim ankles were the ones he remembered. He focused on her eyes once more, seeing the face of a woman, not the girl who'd been his bride all those years ago.

She hadn't moved from the door, looking as if she'd prefer to continue on into the night rather than talk to him. He was so intrigued with the sight of her that he swept that aside. He set down his suitcase and strode over to where she stood, her hand still resting on the door.

"Small world," he said. "What are the odds of us runnin' into each other in a place the size of New York?"

"Nil, I'm sure." She looked thoroughly disconcerted.

Colby glanced at the redhead, who had a thin smile on her lips. "Evenin', ma'am," he said, even though he knew down-home affability wasn't overly appreciated in the Big Apple. But then, he'd always had an rebellious streak in him as wide as the Mississippi.

"This is my friend, Moira McKenzie," Lizzy said, introducing them.

"Pleasure, Ms. McKenzie," he said, removing his hat and taking her thin, gloved hand.

She acknowledged his comment with a nod, mumbling, "How do you do?"

Colby turned his attention back to Lizzy. She was looking at him more out of the corner of her eye than straight on. That wide sensuous mouth of hers, the one he'd once kissed with such pleasure, was pulled into a thin smile like her friend's. Well, once she heard what he'd come to tell her, that smile would most likely be a bit more friendly.

"You rushing off someplace, or do you ladies have time to visit?" he drawled.

She looked at her companion. "Moira and I just finished dinner and we were going to share a taxi home."

"Well, maybe I can talk you both into havin' a drink with me first." He paused for a moment, giving her time to consider his invitation before going on. "I assume you got my letter, by the way."

"Yes, Colby, I did. But I wasn't expecting to hear from you until next week."

"I thought I'd come up a little early and spend the weekend enjoying some of your good restaurants. Maybe take in a show or two, stir up some trouble." He gave Moira a wink.

Lizzy shifted uneasily. "If you can stand the weather, it's a good time to visit, I guess," she said, obviously straining to make conversation. "Not so many tourists."

"I come often enough that that part's not so important."

She blinked. "You're in New York a lot?"

"Several times a year."

"Oh, really."

Her surprise at that amused him. Ten years ago she'd considered him a hick...one with sex appeal, maybe, but a hick. When push had come to shove, she and her rich family had all but run him out of town because he was an embarrassment. And judging by her reaction now, it evidently hadn't occurred to her that he might have changed in the interim. Well, so much the better, he thought. That put him at an advantage.

"I like New York," he explained, "though you might find that hard to believe."

She gave him her little-rich-girl smile. The expression was the same he'd seen a decade earlier, though maybe a tad subtler. He turned to Moira.

"I'm from the Lone Star state, Ms. McKenzie, if you hadn't guessed." He lifted a booted foot, peered down at it, then added, "It only looks like I'm on my way to a costume party."

He gave Lizzy a wink, knowing she was dying inside, which secretly gave him a kick. Not that making her squirm amused him, because he bore her no ill will. But things had been so unequal between them in the past that not giving a damn now was a pleasure.

Still, he wouldn't rub it in. In a few days he'd be facing her across a negotiating table. It would be stupid to complicate things unnecessarily. On the other hand, if Lizzy chose to let their past affect her, he had no problem using it to his advantage.

A couple came in the door just then and the three of them stepped aside to let them pass.

"We seem to be blocking the door. Why don't we find a better place to confabulate?" he said, intentionally choosing the word. "Let me buy you both a drink."

The women looked at each other.

"I can go on alone, Liz," Moira said. "Stay if you like."

"There's no need to run off, Moira," Colby said. "It's not like Lizzy and I have anything private to catch up on." He turned to Lizzy. "She does know that...uh... we..."

She nodded. "Yes, she knows."

Colby grinned, finding more pleasure in this than he'd have expected. His enjoyment went far beyond the irony of the situation, or even catching Lizzy off balance. For reasons he couldn't fully explain, he felt damned good about himself. Maybe it was nothing more than that he was in such a different position than the last time he'd seen her.

The redhead looked at Lizzy as if trying to divine her true desires. Women, he'd discovered, worked together like tag-team wrestlers when dealing with men.

"A cup of coffee?" Lizzy said to Moira.

That was the signal the redhead needed. "Really, you stay, Liz," she said. "To be honest, the champagne gave me a headache. I'm going home and taking a couple of aspirin." She gave Lizzy a hug, then turned, offering her hand. "Nice to have met you. Liz is my best friend so you won't be surprised to hear that I've heard quite a bit about you over the years."

"Oh? Not all bad, I trust."

"Not all." She smiled at them both, patted Lizzy's hand and pushed the door open. "Bye."

"Let me get you a taxi," Colby offered.

"I'll manage, but thanks." And she was gone.

They looked after her, then turned to each other. Lizzy pulled off the beret and ran her fingers through her gold hair, done up in those fashionable ringlets you'd see in the women's magazines. Her expression was uncertain.

"So," she said, "after all these years..."

"Yeah, after all these years."

Colby took another good long look at her and was struck by what he saw. The pretty girl he'd known—the blushing maiden—had become a woman. She regarded him candidly for the first time, showing her courage. Her eyes settled on him. Colby liked the feel, the connection.

"You're prettier than I remembered," he said fearlessly.

"Thank you."

Colby studied her face. She had a great mouth. He liked the sensuality of it. And she knew how to use it. The woman, he recalled, could kiss. Even as a sexual neophyte, she had all the right instincts, a natural passion. Lord, just thinking about it aroused him. "You know, I wondered how it'd feel, seeing you again."

"Oh? How does it feel?"

The question brought a smile. She had a directness that he didn't recall. And courage. Ten years earlier there would have been no telling which way she was headed. His disappointment had been the way she'd fallen so easily under her mother's influence.

"We'll have to discuss that," he said, taking her by the arm. They went to where he'd left his suitcase. "Okay if I check in and get rid of this bag?"

She nodded and he stepped to the registration desk, plopping down his gold card. While the clerk handled the paperwork, Colby glanced back. Lizzy'd taken off her coat. Her clingy blue knit dress showed off her figure. She was riper than before, but still quite slim.

She was a sophisticated, beautiful, classy woman—which usually would have been a source of pleasure for him. But, he reminded himself, Lizzy was his ex, and he couldn't allow himself to be distracted. God knew, he hadn't come to New York for that—at least not with her. He was here to do business. Important business.

When he caught her eye, they exchanged smiles. Damned if he didn't feel vibes between them. He hadn't expected this. Hadn't even considered the possibility. The folks he knew who were divorced mostly hated one another, so he'd assumed there'd be no love lost between them. Of course, the evening was young. There was still plenty of time for hard feelings.

"Mr. Sommers," the clerk said.

Colby turned around.

"If you'll sign here, please."

He signed the form, took the room key and carried his case down to the bell station. Nobody was there, but he signaled to the desk clerk that he was leaving it. Then he sauntered back over to his one-time wife, removing his sheepskin coat.

They studied each other—not as strangers, but rather as long-ago lovers. It was an odd combination of something new and something old.

"What'll it be, Lizzy, coffee or a drink?"

"For starters, please call me Liz. Nobody's called me Lizzy since I was seventeen."

"Old habits die hard," he said with a chuckle. "But I believe you were eighteen, and still my wife, the last time I called you Lizzy. I won't quibble, though. If it's Liz you want, it's Liz you'll get."

"Thank you."

Liz, he judged, was wary. At the same time she was drawn to him and fighting it. He could tell.

"Have a beer with me?" he said, deciding it was time to take charge.

She hesitated. "Do you think it's a good idea?"

"Sure. Why not? I won't bite."

She laughed. "That wasn't always true."

He rolled his tongue through his cheek. "Somehow I think it's best to leave that one alone." He took her arm. "Come on, I'll buy you a drink."

"All right."

They went to the entrance of the lounge. Colby opened the door for her. As she passed by he got a whiff of her sweet, womanly scent, bringing back pleasant recollections of times past.

On many occasions, he'd thought of that first day Liz had showed up at Virgil Gibson's ranch, fresh from the city, her skin pink as a baby's bottom, the collar of her blouse buttoned to the neck with a thin gold chain around it, her chin elevated just so—a feisty little puppy released into the great outdoors for the first time. She'd had a pretty face and a knockout little figure to go with her spirit, a combination that was too damned hard to resist.

Liz turned to see where he wanted to sit. The lounge was nearly deserted. A couple was at a table. Two men were smoking and talking at the bar. Colby guided her to a booth in the far corner. She slid onto the banquette, putting her coat and purse in the middle. He put his briefcase next to it. There was no barmaid in sight, so he decided to get their drinks.

"What'll it be?"

"I suppose I should stick with wine because I've been drinking champagne," she said.

"Been celebrating?"

Liz held up her left hand. For the first time he saw the emerald. Normally a woman's ring finger was the first thing he noticed, but she'd been wearing gloves until she'd taken off her coat.

He controlled his shock well, though it was an unwelcome bit of news. "Looks like we've got catching up to do," he said, not giving the slightest inkling of what he was feeling. "I'll be right back."

He went to the bar with his usual swagger, but there was real disappointment in his gut. It seemed somehow unfair that she should be committed to someone. He didn't like having his expectations raised—if that was an accurate way to put it—only to be deflated.

But something else about it bothered him. Colby tried to figure out what. Then it occurred to him—the incongruity of her behavior. Her mouth said one thing, her eyes another. An engaged woman shouldn't be acting so interested. Of course, he could be misreading her. His inclination was to find out. She'd let him know soon enough if those vibes were real or just meaningless static.

"Have any champagne on ice?" he asked the barman.

"California champagne."

"Give me the best you've got. And a couple of glasses."

Colby glanced back across the lounge. Liz was lost in thought, obviously distracted. Seeing her in profile, the slight upturn of her nose, the delicate line of her jaw, brought recollections flooding back. Suddenly he could recall the taste of her mouth, her scent when they had sex, even the feel of her icy fingers when she'd come running out to the bunkhouse and jumped into his bed.

He absently drummed his knuckles on the bar, contemplating the challenge of finding out just how serious this engagement of hers was. Would that be unfair? he wondered. Maybe, but there was no way he was going to pass up a chance to check out her true feelings. Women who were emotionally involved just didn't send out the kind of signals he'd been sensing—unless, of course, he was misreading her.

He knew better than to jump to conclusions, though. He'd been out in the world long enough to know that the best way to play the game was to let it come to you.

The years had made him a man of considerable practicality. He dealt with the world as he found it, doing what he could to make the best of each situation.

Women had always fascinated him, and he'd enjoyed considerable success with them. And yet, the ease with which he won their affections did not directly translate into peace of mind. Colby was inclined to keep his women at arm's length when it came to emotion, though physical intimacy was never a problem. More than one woman had told him his appeal was as much a curse as a blessing.

Colby had never been a hundred percent sure whether he was wary of getting too involved because he'd been born that way, or because of his fractured marriage to Liz. He'd been inclined to level some of the blame on her, eventually accepting that their relationship had proven to him that he never wanted to go through love and marriage again.

Of course, the way things had ended might have had something to do with it. He'd left town with his tail between his legs, humiliated and hurt. He'd chalked it up to experience—though he'd decided never to be made a fool of again.

And so he couldn't help but be intrigued by the possibility that this encounter was fate giving him a second chance to prove something, to himself and to her. Damned ironic she was engaged. And even more ironic the vibrations between them were as strong as they'd ever been.

Something about that challenged him. He wanted to explore the possibilities, despite her apparent unavailability. No, if he was completely honest, maybe *because* of it.

3

LIZ HAD BEGUN second-guessing herself from the moment Moira had left. True, being with her friends and drinking champagne had already put her in a reckless mood, but the real problem was that Colby had thrown her off balance. Being with him was like a walk back in time. And yet, she didn't feel like the young girl who'd run off to get married on a lark. Instead, she felt like someone else, someone she didn't even know.

Ariel's comment that tonight might be her last chance as a single woman to indulge in some merrymaking had stuck in Liz's mind, as well. True, she'd declined the chance to go barhopping quickly enough. But this was different. Colby wasn't a stranger—at least not in the usual sense. Yet in an odd way she didn't know him at all. Not the man he was now. They'd simply shared a little history.

And the same bed.

The part that concerned Liz most was her state of mind. First, she was feeling the wine. Second, there'd been all the ribald talk with her friends. She had left the meeting feeling empty, aching for something... more...something that was missing in her life. Then who should come along but Colby? It was almost as if she'd been primed to meet up with him.

She glanced over at him. He seemed perfectly prepared for their encounter, as though he'd expected it.

That couldn't be, of course. It was just that Colby was more confident than she'd remembered, more in tune with the real world than before.

A decade earlier, when he'd come to New York for her, Liz had been embarrassed by his naiveté. What had been charming in Texas, seemed obtuse in the context of her social circle. But even though he still wore boots, she could tell he no longer was a wide-eyed innocent. New York had become a place to dine well and take in plays. If anything, he mocked it. Albeit politely.

Simply put, Colby Sommers had grown up. His manliness was more pronounced. He was still rough-hewn, elemental, but these traits were tempered with a confidence, a grace that came with being at peace with himself.

Men in her world simply did not come with Colby's brand of rugged sensuality. In Colby there was a gentleness beneath the calluses and the wry humor. Three minutes with the man and she had seen it all.

And yet, she knew that underneath it all, Colby was still himself. There was nothing false about him. Not ten years ago. Not now. He'd been irresistible then. He was irresistible now.

Liz checked out his body, his jeans-clad legs, the boots, the broad shoulders, and asked herself if she was still opposed to a rowdy night of merrymaking. It shocked her that she could so easily address the temptation. But then Liz had always had a knack for getting to the heart of the matter. That was why she was a good lawyer. "You want to deal, let's deal," she said under her breath.

So, what is it you want, Mr. Sommers? she asked herself as she watched him pay the bartender. *To get re-*

venge? To amuse yourself at my expense? To seduce me? Or just reject me?

Liz shuddered at the memory of running through the snow to the bunkhouse and Colby's warm embrace. She remembered the joy of being surrounded by him. She recalled the expectation as she lay in her bed, knowing he was waiting for her, naked under the coarse sheets and wool blankets.

Liz clenched her fists, angry with herself. She was no longer a virginal teenager. She was engaged to be married. Tomorrow was Valentine's Day. She'd be making dinner for Grayson. How could she demean their love by thinking about sex with a man for whom she had absolutely no feelings?

Colby left the bar and made his way toward her with an ice bucket and a couple of flutes. In her mind's eye Liz could see him ambling across the dusty yard at her dad's ranch, his shirt soaked with perspiration. It was the morning of her second day in Texas. She saw Colby stopping at the edge of the porch and hoisting a booted foot onto the weathered floorboards. "How'd you like to see the horses, Miss Cabot? Virgil tells me you've never been on a working ranch before. Said I should give you a tour." She recalled how warm and large and strong his callused hand had seemed when he'd helped her down from the porch.

Here, now, in New York, Colby loomed over her. "Since champagne seems to be the drink of choice, I thought we could celebrate your engagement and our reunion in style," he said, scooting onto the banquette across from her.

Did he know how incongruous those two things were? she wondered.

More champagne was the last thing she needed, but Liz didn't object. She watched him pour the bubbly then hand her a glass.

"Here's to seeing you again, Lizzy. Oops...I mean, Liz. And to the opportunity to wish you every happiness."

"Thank you."

He gave her a sly wink and touched his glass to hers. They drank. Staring into her eyes, he grinned. It was the grin that had haunted her sleep for years, a grin that said he knew just how things would end.

"As I recall, the last time you got engaged you weren't old enough to drink champagne," he observed.

"I remember."

"So, I guess this is progress."

"A funny choice of words."

"It's certainly not déjà vu."

An image flashed in her mind of Colby kissing her in the barn, practically lifting her off the ground. She'd felt so small and light and helpless in his arms.

"No, it's certainly not."

Liz stared into his pale blue eyes. She noticed little squint lines at the corners that hadn't been there ten years before. And she noticed the slightly weathered look about him. But he was as handsome as ever— more even than she recalled. More compelling, if that was possible.

Colby's dark hair was slightly mussed, the stubble of a long day shaded his strong jaw. The scent of the outdoors, imagined or real, lingered about him. Though her memories of him were distant, the reality was immediate. He seemed terribly familiar, the way something deeply cherished was familiar.

And the way Colby seemed to be reacting to her compounded the effect. It was like she was looking into a mirror and, in seeing him, she was seeing herself. She sensed it was the same for him. They were testing thoughts, savoring memories, their minds working in tandem.

"What's your fiancé's name?" he asked.

"Pardon?"

"Your fiancé. His name?"

"Oh." She blushed. "Grayson. Grayson Bartholomew."

"Hmm...sounds...substantial. What does he do?"

"Grayson's a lawyer, like me."

"Meaning you have a lot in common."

Liz bowed her head.

"Well," he said, touching her glass again, "to you and Grayson."

Colby drained half his champagne and watched her take a sip. He stared at her mouth for a long, long time. It made her heart pound, the way he looked at her. And it made her palms wet. She hadn't reacted to a man this way for...ten years. Liz wanted to hate him, resent him for making her feel the way she did, but she couldn't.

Colby reached out and took her hand, drawing it across the table so he could see her ring. She recalled that first morning in the barn when he'd grabbed her wrist firmly, putting a handful of oats in her palm, and holding her hand steady while his horse lapped up the grain with its coarse wet tongue. She'd shivered that day, as she shivered now. Taking compassion on the little city girl she was, Colby had wiped her palm on the front of his shirt to clean away the horse's frothy spittle.

Her fingers trembled as they lay in his large hand now. The light wasn't good, but he checked out her ring as though it would hold the secret to her feelings about Grayson.

"Nice stone," he said.

"Thank you."

The ring was sizable without being ostentatious. Suitable. Grayson had picked it out himself and it reflected the sort of man he was. Solid. Careful. Proper. Anything but frivolous. Liz didn't love the ring, truth be known, but she liked it very much.

"Grayson must be quite a guy."

"He is," she replied.

"An Ivy League sort of guy, I imagine."

"Frankly, I'd rather not talk about Grayson, if you don't mind."

He gave her a questioning look, then shrugged. "Sure."

Pulling her hand free, she said, "So tell me, are you a rancher these days? Seems to me, Dad's lawyer said something about you having a place of your own."

"Yep. About six or seven miles from Virgil's place."

"It's funny, but when I think about you, I always picture you on Dad's ranch."

"That and leaving town with my tail between my legs, I expect."

Liz shook her head. "No, I don't think of that much."

Colby grinned wryly, as if he didn't believe her. But he didn't say anything. Instead, he pulled the bottle of wine from the ice bucket and added a splash to her glass, then to his own.

"I take it you're still single," she said.

"Yes, I've become cautious in my old age." He chuckled.

Liz took a drink. The bubbles made her nose itch. Colby watched her get a handkerchief from her purse and wipe her nose.

"You look damned good, by the way," he said. "Or have I already said that?"

"You're still full of compliments."

"You know what they say about old dogs," he said. "Time's been good to you, Liz. You're not as cute as you were, but you are a hell of a lot prettier. A fine, handsome woman, as Virgil would say."

She smiled at the mention of her father. "My alienation from Dad was one of the major tragedies of our breaking up. I wish I'd been able to get to know him better before he died."

"He was sorry, too, Liz. And so was I. I felt badly about that."

"It was hardly your fault."

He shrugged. "I made mistakes."

"We all did."

He fingered the stem of his champagne flute. "You know what surprises me most about seeing you again?"

She shook her head.

"I didn't expect to be attracted to you. Ex-wives are supposed to have warts, but I'm sittin' here thinking you're about the most intriguing woman I've ever seen."

"You haven't changed a bit."

"No?"

"You said something like that before you kissed me the first time."

He rolled his tongue through his cheek. "Then I'm either repeatin' myself, or it's still true."

"Could be you're using the same lines you used then."

They exchanged bemused smiles. Liz drank more wine. She was starting to feel tipsy, but didn't object when Colby refilled her glass.

"Can I ask you a direct question?" she said.

"Why not?"

"Did you hate me when I refused to go back to Texas with you?"

"Hate, no. I was deeply disappointed. Hurt. I loved you and it wasn't easy being rejected, especially when I knew you loved me, too."

"That wasn't love, Colby. Our marriage was the irrational act of two self-possessed children in lust."

"You really think it was just hormones? Puppy love?" His voice was very light, as if the question wasn't important.

"We didn't know each other. We weren't fully formed people. We were living out an adolescent fantasy, pretending it was real life."

"I see you have it all figured out," he said. "How long did that take you?" he said, his voice still light.

"Are you being sarcastic, Colby?"

"I'm curious whether your mother's shrink gave that to you, or if you came up with it yourself."

"You *are* being sarcastic."

He gave a self-deprecating laugh. "Forgive me.

Maybe I haven't completely gotten over you dumping me."

"Come on, be honest. After you got home and had a chance to think about it, didn't you think our marriage was a mistake?"

"Maybe I'm too much of a romantic for my own good, but I remember it more fondly than you seem to."

"How *do* you remember it?"

He seemed amused by the conversation. "I think we had something going. There was potential in that marriage."

"Potential," she said, mulling over the word.

"The problem wasn't so much who we were, as the timing. Circumstances weren't ideal."

Liz laughed. "An understatement if I ever heard one. You *are* a romantic, Colby."

"And what are you?"

"A realist."

He shook his head. "I'm not sure I believe that."

"Then maybe you're still naive, after all."

Colby leaned back, crossing his arms as he contemplated her. The repartee seemed to amuse him. The corners of his expressive mouth were turned up slightly. Colby Sommers's every gesture was sexy—and he knew it.

The vibrations between them were getting stronger. They'd been talking about the past, but it was really the present he was testing. If she hadn't found him so darned attractive, it would have been funny to think this was actually happening.

Common sense told her to end it now. She should shift the conversation to business—ask about the oil discovery. She could make an appointment to meet him at the office, then thank him for the drink and catch a cab home. It would be easy. But something held her back.

She wanted to cling to the moment.

Why? Maybe because being with Colby felt so damned good. It had been that way before. It was that way now.

She remembered the single bed in the guest room at her dad's house as the loneliest place on earth. The night wind blowing across the vast Texas wilderness had made her feel forlorn. In the days after her arrival she would lie awake at night, thinking of Colby out in the bunkhouse, knowing that she wanted to be with him, in his bed, in his arms.

The night she'd finally screwed up enough courage to sneak out there seemed, at the time, like the most momentous decision of her life. When he'd opened the door to let her in, there was no need for words, let alone ceremony. She was shivering from cold, her teeth chattering. Colby had hustled her over to the bunk bed and they'd climbed under the covers. He'd held her in his warm embrace. When she'd finally stopped shivering, he'd kissed her. Then he'd made love to her, a ritual they'd repeated several times over the following weeks.

Liz had expected it to get tiresome, expected Colby to lose his allure. Maybe that was why she'd kept at it so relentlessly, to get over him, to prove to herself it wasn't real. But a funny thing happened. She fell in love—or thought she did. By the time her father put a stop to it, she'd realized she couldn't get enough of Colby, which left her no choice but to marry him.

"I don't know if I dare ask what you're thinkin'," he said, rubbing the stubble on his chin. "You have the most wistful look in your eyes."

"I was thinking about the first time we were together," she said brazenly. "Remembering it fondly."

Liz managed to keep a level gaze, knowing the champagne was talking for her. That was okay, though. It made doing what she wanted to do easier.

His reaction was guarded. He seemed to be weighing the implications of her comment. "I'm pleased to hear it," he said, "especially considering I've got fond recollections of my own."

She wasn't going to ask about them. Instead, she gazed into his eyes and asked herself the most important question of all: Could she make love with Colby again and still marry Grayson?

Wendy had told her she should have a fling to get other men out of her mind. Until now, Liz would have said it was a stupid idea. And maybe it was stupid, but Colby at least made her think about it.

She drank more champagne even though her head was already spinning and her tongue was getting much too loose for her own good. She held out her glass for him to fill. Colby obliged.

"I guess I don't have to tell you how damned sexy you are," she said. "It'd only make your head swell."

He carefully put the bottle back in the ice bucket. "Are you trying to compliment me, Lizzy? Or was that an insult?"

"I'm not sure. I'm tipsy."

"And therefore not responsible for what you say?"

"Now who's doing the insulting?"

"I prefer to think of it as affectionate chiding," he said drolly.

"Affectionate chiding," she grumbled. "You're just trying to give me a hard time because of what I did ten years ago."

"So, we *are* making progress."

She studied him with genuine admiration. "You've got it down to a science, you know that?"

"I've got what down to a science?"

"Being a suave, macho, sexy cowboy. You were dynamite in bed at twenty-three, so you must be a grand master by now."

"Another compliment."

She quaffed some wine. "Exactly."

"To what end, if you don't mind me asking?"

She shrugged, unable to say it. Colby, showing compassion, took her hand. Liz didn't move. Instead, she watched him gently caress her fingers, the way he used to.

It frightened her, and she suddenly realized she'd gone too far. Much too far. "I should go," she said.

"Yes, you probably should."

She heard the words but even as he said them, he continued caressing her fingers.

"Do you want me to go?"

"No, I'd rather you stay."

"Why?"

"Why do you think?" he said.

"If I do, will you behave yourself?"

"The more relevant question is, will you?"

She laughed, then drank more champagne.

"That was a serious question," he said.

Liz gazed at his hand, watching it make love to hers.

"You're asking what my intentions are," she murmured.

"To be blunt about it, I guess I am."

"You know, of course, that by putting me on the spot, you may be forcing my hand," she said. "I may have no choice but to leave."

"Maybe."

Colby repeatedly ran his finger around her engagement ring as though exorcising a demon. It was painful for her to watch, so she freed her hand, pulled the ring off her finger and slipped it into her purse, then met his gaze.

He looked at her as though he was expecting an explanation. She said nothing until it became obvious he had no intention of asking why she'd done that. "I didn't feel comfortable watching you touch Grayson's ring," she finally said.

Colby took her hand and cupped it in his like it was a baby bird he was protecting. His touch made her shiver.

"I'd much rather caress your hand than some other guy's ring, Liz."

"That 'other guy' is the man I'm going to marry."

"So you've said."

"I'm serious."

"I believe you," Colby said. "And I think Grayson would be pleased to hear it, too."

Liz gave him a look, pulling her hand free. "You know, I don't know if you're so damned appealing because you're a bastard, or in spite of it."

"Does it matter?"

Colby took the wine bottle and split the last of the

champagne between their glasses. He drank and so did she. Neither spoke.

Colby knew he had her.

And so did she.

"You know what I'm thinking now?" she asked, surrendering what resistance she may have had left.

He shook his head.

"I'm remembering that day at the ranch a couple of weeks after I arrived. You'd gone out early to hunt and I saw you at a distance, riding back across the prairie. There was a thin layer of snow on the ground. It was midmorning. I was at the kitchen window, watching. You and your horse were breathing hard, big puffs of vapor coming from your mouths with each breath."

She smiled, shaking her head.

"It was the most romantic sight I'd ever seen. A handsome cowboy on horseback. The sun gleaming. That night was the first time I sneaked out to the bunkhouse."

He studied her, the hint of a self-satisfied smile playing at the corners of his mouth.

"You must have known how crazy I was about you," she said.

"I had a pretty good idea when you knocked on the bunkhouse door that night."

"Do you remember it? *Really* remember it, I mean?"

"I can still recall the taste of your mouth, Liz, the feel of your skin, the hard nubs of your breasts against my bare chest. Yes, I remember it. Like it happened last night."

She swallowed hard and looked down, no longer able to meet his gaze. "I guess you do," she said under her breath.

"It was a special night," he said.

Liz nodded. Colby took her hand again, this time rubbing her knuckles. The strength of his grip had an electric effect. She took a deep breath, recalling the moment he entered her, the terrible and wonderful experience she'd waited for.

Even though she'd been a virgin, she hadn't been afraid. At least not much. Ironically, she was feeling a greater fear of the unknown now, ten years and thousands of miles later.

Liz knew what she wanted. She just wasn't sure how to ask for it. Colby's pride wouldn't allow him to proposition her. It was up to her.

She thought for a moment, testing her courage as she tried to balance desire against pride, strength against weakness, the past against the future. Then, gathering herself, she said it. "I want that night again, Colby," she whispered. "I want you to take me to your room."

He reached out and touched her cheek. She looked into his eyes, wanting him to understand her need without judging her.

"I know it's stupid and selfish and wrong," she said, "but it's what I want." Her lip trembled.

He contemplated her words. It infuriated her that he didn't say yes, or for that matter, no.

"I just want to know one thing, Lizzy," he finally drawled. "Is this you talkin', or is it the champagne?"

"I want to be with you," she said. "That's all I know."

"Just for tonight, I take it."

"Yes, just for tonight."

Colby looked at his watch. "How can I turn down a

lady on her birthday? Especially when her birthday also happens to be Valentine's Day."

"This also would have been our tenth anniversary," she said. "Were you aware of that?"

He gave her his most seductive look. "Sweetheart, how could I forget?" He pulled her hand to his lips and kissed it. Then he slipped from the booth, grabbing his coat. He extended his hand. "Come on. I'm as eager as you are to find out if the magic's still there."

Liz gathered her things and slid from the booth. Colby held her hand as they returned to the hotel lobby. She went to wait by the elevators while he fetched his case. After picking it up, he made a detour to the registration desk. Liz couldn't see what he was doing until the clerk took a long-stemmed red rose from the vase on the desk and handed it to him. Colby gave the man a bill, then made his way to the elevators.

"This is for you," he said, handing her the rose. "A token of remembrance."

Her eyes bubbled as she pressed the blossom to her nose. When the tears started rolling down her cheeks, Colby dug a handkerchief from his pocket and gave it to her. Liz wiped her eyes.

"I've obviously had too much to drink," she said. "I'm not myself tonight."

"Don't go saying that, or I'll put you in a taxi and send you home." He gave her a stern look. "I'm serious."

The elevator arrived. They peered into the empty car.

"What's it going to be, Liz? The snowy streets of New York or my warm bed?"

Liz sighed, the pull of the waiting elevator stronger

than the pull of the main hotel door behind her. After
only a brief hesitation, she marched into the elevator
and leaned resolutely against the back railing. Colby
followed her in, but held the doors open with one
hand.

"You're sure?"

"Let the door close," she said. "You know how I hate
winter."

Colby let go of the door. He pushed the button for
his floor and moved next to her as the elevator car rose.
Liz looked up at him, towering over her. After a moment he took her chin in his hand, leaned down and
kissed her softly.

With her eyes closed, the elevator seemed to spin, as
well as rise. Her heart pounded. The kiss ended as the
car came to a stop. Liz took a deep breath.

"Hard to believe it's been ten years," he said.

She took his arm and they stepped into the hallway.
"Don't say another word, Colby," she said. "I don't
want to think about anything. I just want to be in your
bed one more time."

4

COLBY OPENED THE DOOR to his room and turned on the light. "Ma'am," he said, gesturing for her to step in. He tossed his hat and jacket on a nearby chair.

Liz entered, looking around. Then she went to the window, where she gazed out at New York by night. A siren wailed in the distance as she nervously tossed her things behind her, on the big bed. Colby could tell she was fighting herself and he didn't want to crowd her. So he waited, still standing by the door.

After a long time, she turned to him. Her expression was carefully blank. He could tell she was upset. "You all right, Lizzy?"

She shook her head. "No."

"What's the matter? Second thoughts?"

"Yes," she said, lowering her head.

"This door works both ways. You can go out as easily as you came in."

She took a deep breath, and when she spoke her voice was shaky. "I'm acting like a fool, I know."

"Listen, sweetheart, if you don't want to do this, you can head on home. People change their minds all the time. Don't let it bother you."

"I feel guilty as hell."

Colby appraised her, rubbing his jaw. "It's your decision."

She started to say something, but she must have

thought better of it because she stopped herself. It was a full minute before she finally spoke again. "I'm sorry to have put you through this."

Colby walked over to the window and gently took her chin so that she had to look up at him. He gave her his most reassuring smile. "No hard feelings," he said.

"You're very generous, Colby." Liz lowered her eyes. "I really did think I wanted to go to bed with you."

"But now you've come to your senses."

"I'm no less attracted to you than I was five minutes ago. It's just that..."

"...everything has its price," he said, finishing the sentence for her.

"Yes, I guess that's what it comes down to."

Colby was not surprised. If a woman didn't change her mind every now and again, she'd lose her privileges. He could see it was a situation that called for compassion. And a little assertiveness on his part.

"Okay, princess," he said, getting her coat from the bed and holding it for her. She slipped it on and he carefully buttoned it. Then he set her beret on her head, adjusting it at a rakish angle. She looked adorable. "I'm taking you back downstairs and putting you in a cab. No sense beating ourselves. We had a nice chat. The evening wasn't a waste."

Liz somehow managed to look disappointed. That didn't surprise him, either.

He glanced around. "Where are your gloves?"

"In my pocket."

"Put them on."

She obeyed. Then she stood there, gazing up at him like a reluctant child. She seemed so unhappy, so vulnerable. The pain in his heart reminded him how much he'd once loved her.

"You look like an angel, sugar, whether you feel like one or not." He leaned over and kissed her lightly on the lips. Then he opened the door and took her hand. "Come on."

They went into the hall. He led her to the elevator. He could tell she was having second thoughts. Again.

"I should have kept my mouth shut and just done it," she groaned. "That way neither of us would have had to deal with this frustration."

"Guilt is better?"

"I feel guilty anyway. What kind of woman comes this close to betraying her fiancé?"

"You didn't betray anyone."

"I wanted to."

The elevator arrived. Colby motioned for her to enter the car and followed her in.

"I'd feel better if you hated me a little," she said.

"Well, I am sort of annoyed. Does that help?"

She watched the lights on the floor-indicator panel. Colby looked at her pretty mouth, his disappointment deepening.

"I'll probably tell Grayson about this," she said as the car came to the ground floor and the doors slid open.

"That'll make him feel wonderful, I'm sure."

"Wouldn't you want to know?" She stepped into the lobby.

Colby wavered between a diplomatic response and the truth. He opted for the latter. "I never plan on being in a situation like this. I would hope that any woman I was engaged to wouldn't *want* to take my ring off her finger."

She colored and they started toward the door.

"You're embarrassed now, I know," he said, "but these things pass. I didn't exactly feel like Napoleon when you and your mother ran me out of town."

"You got paid twenty-five thousand."

He glanced over at her, surprised she picked this particular moment to bring that up. "Yes, but after the fact."

"You kept it."

They stopped at the entrance, on the spot where they'd bumped into each other an hour earlier.

"You're right," he said, facing her. "I kept it. I figured if I was going to get screwed, I might as well have something to show for it. As far as I'm concerned, our accounts are square now."

Liz extended her hand in a businesslike fashion. "Good. I'll accept that," she said, not sounding sincere. "I take it you'll call me on Monday."

"That was the plan."

Liz turned up the collar of her coat and stared up at him. "There's no reason for you to go outside. You don't have a coat."

"I'm getting you safely into a cab, so don't argue." They went outside, the blast of cold air hitting him like ice water. A couple of taxis went by, but both had fares. He moved into the street, ignoring the snow blowing in his face.

"It'll serve you right if you catch pneumonia," she said. "You should have stayed inside like I told you."

"Compassion was never one of your strong points, Lizzy."

Up at the corner he spotted a free taxi on the cross street. Colby put his fingers to his mouth and let out a shrill whistle, then waved his arms. The cab driver made a last-minute turn and came toward them. Colby stepped back onto the curb. He gave Liz a wink. She did not look pleased.

When the taxi pulled up, he stepped into the street and opened the rear passenger door.

Liz stepped off the curb, looking up at him. She didn't get into the cab. "Just answer me this," she said, "honestly. Did you want me tonight?"

Colby pinched her cheek. "Silly question."

He shivered and Liz reached up, pulling his face down to hers. She kissed him violently, albeit briefly. Her eyes were shimmering as she turned and got into the taxi.

He closed the door and returned to the curb. The vehicle pulled away. The last thing he saw was Liz Cabot's blurry image in the steamy window of the cab. He went inside.

Though warm, the lobby of the hotel seemed alien. There was no one around but the desk clerk, who gave him a perfunctory nod as he strode to the elevator bank. Colby got in the car they'd come down in. He rubbed his arms. The fabric of his shirt felt icy. As the doors closed, he leaned his head against the side of the car and watched the floor-indicator lights hop across the panel. He could almost smell the remnants of Liz's perfume. It made him vaguely sad. He wished she hadn't kissed him at the end. But then, maybe she was entitled to the last word.

Colby chuckled to himself. Liz Cabot still drove him crazy. Maybe worse than ever. He strode down the hall to his room. Like the lobby, it seemed alien and forbidding. He would have much preferred to be at home with a roaring fire. The only option was TV—if he could take the usual nightly dose of murders on the late news. Deciding against it, he headed for the bath.

As he passed the bed, he noticed Liz's rose on the spread. He picked it up and took a sniff. A twinge went through him, a twinge of nostalgia that he didn't particularly like—not now.

Colby went to the wastebasket with the intent of tossing the flower away, then thought better of it. Instead, he got a water glass from the bathroom, filled it from the tap and put the rose in it, placing the glass on the bedstand. Maybe instead of trying to hide from his feelings, he'd do well to face them.

He stared at the flower for a while, remembering their wedding night with a certain fondness, then he began unbuttoning his shirt. He went into the bathroom and started running a bath.

He was studying his grizzled jaw in the mirror when he heard a rap at the door. He checked his watch, incredulous that a maid would be coming so late to turn down the spread. It was almost midnight.

Colby went to the door, opening it without compunction. It was Liz.

"I forgot my rose," she said apologetically, only then noticing his bare chest.

"You came back for a flower?"

"Only partly," she said, taking a deep breath. "Before I say another word, I want you to know I'm not trying to drive you crazy. I really did think I should leave.... It's just that..." She threw herself into his arms. "Oh, Colby, I want you so much."

"Lizzy, listen..."

She buried her face in his chest and wound her arms around his waist. "I know I deserve it, but please don't send me away. It's Valentine's Day, my birthday...our anniversary. And I do want you. Please say you want me, too."

Colby took a deep breath, inhaling her scent, telling himself that she might be his ex-wife and she might be the woman he was going to have to face across a bargaining table in the next few days, but right then, at that moment, he didn't care about any of that, because Lizzy Cabot was also the most desirable woman he'd ever known. And she wanted him.

LIZ HELD HER BREATH, hoping he wouldn't push her away. And when he leaned down and sweetly kissed her, her heart ached with a longing she hadn't felt in a decade. She reveled in his kiss, giving herself up to it. He nibbled at the corner of her mouth until she parted her lips for him.

She ran her hands up his back, remembering the feel of him, the way it had been. Colby seemed just familiar enough that she could relax, yet unfamiliar enough that she felt an edge. Not enough to make her afraid, just more alive than usual.

With an urgency that surprised her, Colby ran his tongue across her lips and teeth and gums. In response, she flicked her tongue against his, and when he moaned she felt a surge of power. That was the way it had always been between them—each had given, each had taken.

And when their kiss ended, and he picked her up and carried her to the bed and began undressing her,

her thoughts flew back to the first time they'd made love—when she'd gone to the bunkhouse and thrown herself at him.

Even though she'd been a virgin, she'd known that he was the man she wanted for her first time. It had been nearly as easy to make the decision to return to the hotel tonight, because she had not really wanted to leave. Maybe that made her brave; maybe it made her a fool. All she could say for sure was that she had to be with Colby Sommers.

She sighed as he pulled her panty hose down off her legs and tossed them on the floor. Her panties quickly followed, and then her bra. It had always been like that with him. One moment he'd be fiddling with a button on her blouse, and the next thing she knew he'd taken off her clothes and was making love with her.

Liz watched as he got off the bed and began unfastening his pants. The light was still on, and even though she was nude and hadn't been with him for a decade, it seemed natural to watch as he took off his pants and socks and shorts. He stared at her mouth and breasts and hips—refreshing his memory of her.

Suddenly Colby froze, then turned and sprinted for the bath. "Damn it. I left the water running."

As he left the room, she took the opportunity to turn out the light by the bed. Then she noticed that he'd put her rose in the glass of water. She plucked the bud from the makeshift vase and was pressing it to her nose when he returned.

"I was just in time," he said.

"Good. I see you saved my flower," she said, smiling up at him.

He crawled in next to her. "Yep."

"Why?"

"Just because...."

The ambient light from outside cast a silvery green glow on his skin. He took the flower from her hand and kissed her lips, lightly at first, and then with more pressure. Liz leaned back against the pillow. "Oh, Colby, it's been so long...."

"It was just a moment ago, sugar. None of the time in between counts."

He began making love to her in earnest then, kissing her neck and shoulders until she was breathless. Then still holding the flower in one hand, he touched the rosebud to her jawline and between her breasts, lingering to skim each nipple before he took one hardened nub in his mouth and began swirling his tongue around it.

Lizzy ran her hand through his hair, holding his head to her breast. She recalled clearly the first time Colby had done this to her—she had felt a pang of desire and a rush of warm fluid between her legs. And she'd been eager for him to take her, even though a small part of her had been afraid.

She felt the same desire now, only without the fear. All she cared about, all she wanted, was to have Colby Sommers again. To make love with him.

"Oh, God," she said breathlessly as his tongue painted a trail of moisture from her breasts to her thighs.

"You taste just the same," he whispered. "Happy Valentine's Day, sweetheart."

Colby moved lower on the bed, his tongue tracing a line across her stomach to her mound. His touch sent an electric shock through her.

"And happy birthday," he murmured.

Liz moaned as he parted her thighs and kissed her, his tongue delicately tracing the edge of her feminine lips. She bunched the covers in her fists and spread her legs wider as he pleasured her, making her insides quiver.

He'd done this to her the very first time. The wind had howled outside, making the windows rattle. Inside the New York hotel, they were insulated against the elements, the only sign of life the low hum of traffic in the street far below.

As a seventeen year old she had let Colby do with her as he wished. It was different now. She was ready and she wanted him to take her. "Now, Colby," she muttered, "take me now."

He didn't accommodate her immediately, nibbling at her sensitive nub, running his tongue along the inside of her thigh before skimming her lips again.

"I want you," she said more demandingly. "Don't torture me."

"You consider this torture?"

When he pulled back to look down at her, she grasped his shoulders and gazed into his shadowy eyes, her heart pounding a mile a minute, her insides warm and creamy. He must have known that he'd teased her long enough because he moved over her and entered her then. It was a relief. She'd been primed for this even before she saw him climb out of the taxi. She'd been ready for Colby ever since they'd parted. But until that moment, she hadn't realized that he was the only man to excite her this way. In her mind, Colby and sex had become synonymous.

She wrapped her legs around him, arching her back.

Her orgasm rose out of nowhere, overtaking her before she fully realized what had happened. She writhed against him, bringing him with her.

Colby groaned and thrust deep. He stopped undulating within moments, but the throbbing continued. She was so overwhelmed, she began to cry. That had never happened before.

He pulled back to see her face. Liz wiped her eyes.

"You okay, sugar?"

She nodded, sniffling. "Yes," she said in a small voice, "I just got overwhelmed, that's all."

"Which of us gets the credit?" he asked, pressing his face into her hair, inhaling her scent.

Liz put her hand to his cheek. "We both do. Colby, you're fabulous."

He kissed her chin and rolled off of her and onto his back. Liz felt a sudden emptiness that quickly faded when he took her hand. Colby faced her, propping his head on his hand. He touched his finger to her lower lip. Liz lay very still. She was afraid to speak because she didn't know what to say.

What kind of words could explain the way she felt? She did not know. She only knew that something special had happened, a kind of miracle. Fate had brought her into Colby's arms again, and making love with him had been a precious gift.

After a stretch of silence, he began caressing her stomach. His hands were callused, rugged. She had always found his touch sexy. He had often claimed that she could come at the drop of a hat. But that wasn't true—at least not with anyone else. So it had to be Colby. It seemed to her he would turn on any woman.

Or was it just the way they were with each other? Something in the chemistry?

Aroused again, she ran her hand down over his stomach and through the tangle between his legs. She found him erect, making her heart lift.

"I want to be on top this time," she purred.

"All right, sugar, it's your show."

Liz got astride him, guiding his sex deep inside her. Her excitement came even more quickly this time, especially when he began caressing her nipples.

"Oh," she said, moaning. "We're going to do this all night, aren't we?"

"You're not eighteen anymore, and I'm not twenty-three. On the other hand, it's been a while, and I'm not sure I can get all I need of you, even if we do make love all night."

Colby pulled her down over him so he could suck her nipples. Almost at once she was on the edge again. When she sat back upright, he grasped her hips, forcing her into a gallop, and she came quickly, crying like a mewling calf. It was a term Colby had used once to describe her excitement. His climax immediately followed hers.

Spent, she collapsed onto his moist chest and lay there, their hearts pounding. She kissed his neck and purred softly.

"Are you glad I came back?" she whispered.

He trailed his fingers through her curls. "Being a gentleman, I'll let you draw your own conclusions." He continued stroking her hair. "Maybe the more relevant question is, are *you* glad?"

Liz laid her head on his shoulder and sighed. "I can't

think of any place on earth I'd rather be." And it was true, absolutely true. But it was only part of the story. The rest she didn't want to think about. Not now.

5

February 14

THE RAIN DRUMMED against the windowpane. It was the kind of downpour that her father said made the creeks rise, washing out roads. Then it stopped suddenly—so suddenly that Liz sat up in bed, her heart thumping.

After a moment or two, she realized she wasn't in Texas at all. Nor was this her bedroom at home. It was Colby Sommers's room at the Clairbourne. And that wasn't rain she'd heard. It was the shower, and it had stopped. She blinked at the swirling snow outside the window and listened to Colby softly humming some country-and-western tune in the bathroom.

Liz looked at the clock on the bedstand as she rubbed her throbbing temples. Lord, it was nearly nine o'clock! She was due at the office in ten minutes!

Snatching the phone, she punched out the number of Krantz, Markham & Warren. "Molly, it's Liz," she said to the receptionist. "Give me Westley, will you?" After a moment her legal secretary came on the line. "Wes, it's Liz. I'm going to be late. Tell Frank, Alex and Marcia to go ahead without me."

"All right. Shall I say you'll be in before the meeting's over?" he asked.

"I don't know. I mean, I'm not sure I'll be there in

time." She sighed. "Oh, tell them probably not," she added, feeling the need to be decisive. "I'll have to get briefed later."

"Check."

"I should be there by ten-thirty." Liz glanced up and saw Colby at the bathroom door. He had a towel wrapped around his waist but was otherwise naked.

"Okay," Westley said. "Anything you want me to do?"

"Do I have any messages?"

Colby was admiring her naked body. She casually pulled up the sheet to cover her breasts.

"Grayson came by to see when you were due in," her secretary said. "He said to tell you happy birthday, and he wants you to buzz him when you arrive."

Liz turned red at the mention of Grayson's name. "Do me a favor and tell him I got tied up. I'll see him when I get in."

"Check."

"Thanks, Wes."

"Happy birthday, by the way," he said.

"Thank you. See you soon."

She put the phone back in the cradle and turned her full attention to Colby. He was watching her, his arms folded across his broad chest. The happy expression on his face fell short of gloating, but he certainly looked self-satisfied.

"I overslept, and I'm late for work," she said, clutching the sheet to her chest.

"I wasn't sure whether I should wake you or not."

"I wish you had."

"Surely you won't get fired."

"No, but it's not very professional."

"Since you're going to be late anyway, shall I order up breakfast?"

She shook her head. "No, as it is, I'm going to be pressed to get home, shower and change and still be there by ten-thirty."

"Have your shower here. The water's nice and hot."

"I'll still have to change. If I show up wrinkled, in the same outfit I wore yesterday, people will notice."

"I realize now there are advantages to ranching," he said wryly. "By the way, happy Valentine's Day and happy birthday."

"Thank you."

"Dare I mention our anniversary?"

"I'd rather not think about that, to be honest."

"Is there a problem?"

Colby waited, but she didn't respond. She didn't have time for casual chitchat or for beating around the bush. They were dancing around the real issue—namely, what last night meant and what would happen next.

During the night, they'd made love a third time. Colby had taken her from behind, collapsing on her when they'd finally come. Then he'd rolled her onto her side, her body cupped in his, his strong arms around her as he'd kissed her hair and shoulder. She'd lain in his embrace for a long time, thinking about what had happened, even as his breathing had slipped into a soft snore.

The sex had been fabulous. Looking at him now, she wanted to make love again. But her rambling thoughts in the night had eventually led to the implications of what she'd done.

The situation was clear. She'd gone to bed with

Colby because he was a fabulous lover, she had fond memories of him and she wanted to experience him again. Still even though she and Colby had a past, this interlude was basically the anonymous sex Wendy had talked about—simply something that happened one night.

Even as she'd lain in Colby's arms, she'd told herself that it was Grayson who mattered. But how did she really feel about her fiancé? Had things changed? Did she still love him?

Liz was disturbed by her betrayal. She felt guilty, yes, but mostly she was ashamed of her self-indulgence, and being weak. Grayson would understand an indiscretion, though. He was capable of seeing it for what it was—so long as she was clear about describing exactly what had happened and why. When he knew for certain that Colby meant nothing to her, then Grayson would dismiss what had happened. Not that he'd be indifferent. He'd hurt. But it wouldn't be fatal because Grayson was mature enough to take the long view, and keep things in perspective.

"I would take your contemplative silence to be a good sign, sugar," Colby said, "but long ago I learned that with you it is not wise to jump to conclusions. Anything we need to discuss?"

"Right now the most urgent thing on my mind is going to the bathroom."

He smiled. "Shall I avert my eyes while you get up?"

"This *is* the morning after, Colby, and I'm embarrassed as hell. I don't see any point in pretending otherwise."

"As a gentleman, I should have foreseen the problem. Forgive me." He went to the window and gazed

out at the snowy morning, his back to her. "Not exactly
a blizzard, but appears we've got some snow. Traffic
seems to be movin'. I reckon you won't have any trouble getting home."

Liz gathered up her clothes as he talked, then hurried past him to the bathroom. The door closed, she put
her things on the vanity and examined herself in the
mirror. She looked as bad as she felt. The wine had
given her a pounding headache. Her skin was puffy.
Worst, though, were the whisker burns on her chin and
cheeks. Even her chest and shoulders were covered
with splotchy patches of red. She'd scarcely noticed
Colby's beard while they were making love, but for another day or two at least she'd bear the evidence of
their lovemaking.

After going to the bathroom, she rinsed her face with
cold water and patted it dry. She untangled her hair,
then put a spot of Colby's toothpaste on her finger and
rubbed her teeth. Using his toothbrush wouldn't have
been unthinkable, considering, but she'd already decided this was a different day that required a completely new frame of mind.

While lying awake during the night, she'd gotten
Colby in perspective and refocused her thoughts on
Grayson. She would need time to recover from this un-
settling experience; she might even have to make a
confession, but that definitely was the direction she intended to go. Colby Sommers was simply an aberra-
tion, a meaningless dalliance, a fit of self-indulgence.

Quickly dressing, Liz made another attempt to do
something with her hair, then gave up, going back into
the bedroom. She found Colby half-dressed. He had on

clean crisp jeans, gray snakeskin boots and was slipping on a freshly pressed Western shirt.

"Give me a minute and I'll go down to the lobby with you," he said. "Then, after I get you safely in a taxi, I'll grab some breakfast."

"It's not necessary to get me a taxi," she said, using her best lawyer voice. "It's broad daylight and your Texas chivalry is out of place in New York. Sorry, but it's true."

"Yes, I believe I learned that lesson ten years ago. Old habits die hard."

"Yes, I know." She rubbed her arms, feeling both nostalgia and regret. "So I'll say goodbye," she said.

He gave her an appraising look. "You really do mean goodbye. Not so long."

Liz sighed. "I think the kindest thing under the circumstances is to be brutally frank. As far as I'm concerned, last night was just a fling, a last hurrah before marriage. Nothing more."

She waited as he considered her words. He did not look pleased, though she couldn't say he was angry. If anything it was sober reflection.

"I hope it doesn't hurt you that I feel that way," she said. "Neither of us made promises. I was straightforward about what I wanted."

"I hope you weren't disappointed," he said stiffly as he finished buttoning his shirt.

"No, you're the consummate lover. Even better than before."

"So we both had a good time. That's nice to know."

"Look, I know you're bitter. I don't blame you, but—"

"Wait a minute," he said, cutting her off, "I'm not

bitter. And I'm not complaining. As you correctly pointed out, nobody made any promises."

"Then why are you upset?"

"Maybe because I'm feeling some hostility from you that I don't think I deserve."

Liz blinked, but saw that he had a point. "Look, this is not an easy situation for either of us. I'm trying to be as direct and honest as I can. If I've been brusque or insensitive, that was not my intention."

"No need for apologies," he said, tucking in his shirt. "No damage done. Over the years I've learned to develop a very short memory about things like this. We can forget about last night if that's what you want, but we still have to consider our business relationship. That is why I came to New York."

Colby took a string tie from the dresser and put it on as he waited for her response. She took a moment to reflect.

"Okay, maybe we should address that," she said. "I've given it some thought. If you want to buy my interest in Dad's land, it's yours. Tell me what my half is worth and you can have it for that."

"It's not that simple, Liz. There's a lot more at stake than you think."

"Look, I don't care about the property. I don't even want to talk about it. Not now nor later."

"You're being hasty. You haven't heard what I've got to say."

"I don't have time. I really have to go." She headed for the door.

"We're talking a lot of money," he said. "The land is secondary. The mineral rights are what's valuable."

She turned on her heel. "Apparently you don't understand. I don't want to do business with you. I made a terrible mistake going to bed with you, and I want to put it behind me. I have no desire to see you again. Ever. I know that's harsh, but it's the truth. I take full responsibility for what happened. I'm not blaming you. But I'm within my rights to end this here and now and that's exactly what I intend to do."

"You owe it to yourself to listen to me."

She put her hands on her hips. She was getting angry. "This is the last I'm going to say anything about this, then I'm going. I'm giving you my interest in the property, Colby. Did you hear me? *Giving* it to you! You don't have to pay me a cent. It's yours, free gratis. Have your lawyer send me a quitclaim deed and I'll sign everything over to you. The land, the mineral rights, everything."

"That's insane."

"It's what I want. But there is a condition. You can't ever contact me again. That's my price. I want to sever all connections with the past."

"Forgive me, but you're being a bit overly dramatic, Liz. I don't think I've imposed myself or interfered in your affairs."

"It's not what you've done—it's how I feel. When I leave this room, I want to forget this happened. It'll be easier if I never see you again."

He nodded, showing disgust. "All right. You win."

"Thank you."

"I take it you'd rather I not ride down in the elevator with you."

She was shaking from her emotion, much of which had nothing to do with her father's ranch. The utter stupidity of what she'd done in sleeping with him finally had come crashing down on her. Now all she wanted was to get as far away from Colby Sommers as she could. Maybe brutal frankness was the only way to get across the depth of her feelings.

"No," she said as calmly as she could, "I'd like to say goodbye now. Forever," she added, her voice cracking.

He looked resigned. "All right," he said with a casual wave of his hand. "Goodbye, Liz. Have a happy birthday and a nice Valentine's Day."

She lowered her eyes. "Thank you." Then she reached for the doorknob. "I'm sorry about this, Colby, but it's the way it has to be."

"I understand."

She hesitated, glancing his way for the last time, strangely savoring the sight of him, hating what was happening. "Enjoy your stay in New York."

"I'll do my darnedest," he said with a crooked, but vaguely sad smile.

She opened the door.

"So long," he said.

She went into the hall and was halfway to the elevator banks before the tears began flowing down her cheeks. It was like this ten years ago, when he'd climbed into his pickup and driven away. She'd cried the whole day. Then, over the ensuing months, she had redefined her life. This time, hopefully, it would be easier. All she had to do was to forget one night.

BY THE TIME the slender brunette with the big hoop earrings had brought him his coffee, the sun had broken through the clouds and angled into the conference room some sixty floors above the streets of Manhattan.

The woman gave him a flirtatious smile, again checking out his Western garb.

"Sure you don't care for a pastry, Mr. Sommers?"

"No thank you, darlin'," he said affably. "I've had my oatmeal this mornin'."

She gave him another smile and went to the door of the conference room. "Mr. Harris and Mr. Wilhelm will be with you shortly."

"Thank you."

There was a little extra lift in her step as she walked along the other side of the glass wall separating the conference room from the reception area. Colby had flirted with her upon his arrival at Continental American Oil, partially out of habit, partly to salve his bruised ego. He'd always enjoyed bantering with a pretty woman, even when the flirtation was meaningless. The simple fact was, he liked the fairer sex.

Yet, he was painfully aware that it'd take more than a little happy talk to heal his wounded pride. He'd hardly expected Liz to profess her undying love, but he'd figured that a more measured, realistic response was in order. Her desire never to see him again struck him as excessive—particularly when he had made no demands. To react so harshly, and with such passion, could only mean one thing. She was afraid.

Colby wasn't sure what that meant. Either she feared for her future with her fiancé, or she feared him. And if it was him that she feared, was it because of what he might do, or what *she* might do?

Colby could forgive her weaknesses, but the unceremonious way in which she'd dumped him brought back unpleasant memories. Of course, that was *his* problem. Liz probably didn't realize he was carrying scars from the past, that his utter humiliation at the hands of her family still weighed on him. Or maybe she did realize it, and simply didn't want to put herself in the position of being the object of revenge.

Colby shook his head. Could Liz actually believe that their lovemaking had been an act of retribution? He didn't see how. True, there'd been a certain satisfaction in knowing the woman who had rejected him ten years before had wanted him to make love last night. But that was secondary. The Liz Cabot of today was of far greater interest than the Liz Cabot of yesterday.

Ironically, he hadn't given it a lot of thought while they were together. He'd simply enjoyed the moment, being with her. While he showered he'd wondered what frame of mind morning would find her in—stoic acceptance or painful embarrassment. He'd half expected a plea to pretend that it hadn't happened, but not a demand that he never darken her door.

Colby's first impulse was to say the hell with her. After all, he had as much claim to indignation as she. If anyone had been used, he had the stronger case. But that was okay. He'd gone into it with his eyes open.

Even so, he didn't like the implication that he was somehow a threat or a danger, that he had to be held at bay. If he was a problem to her, it wasn't his fault. Which brought him back to the idea that Liz might be afraid of her own feelings.

The door to the conference room opened. Two men entered, one about Colby's age, the other eight or ten years older. The senior was Ed Wilhelm, the vice president of domestic operations for Continental American. He introduced Tom Harris, head of the mineral rights acquisitions division. Wilhelm motioned for

Colby to take a seat. Both men joined him on the same side of the table.

"Are you enjoying your stay in New York?" Wilhelm said, pushing his rimless glasses up off his nose.

"Just got in last evening. First night was a good one."

"You're staying at the Clairbourne, aren't you?"

"Yes."

"Well located. Not far from the theater district, lots of good restaurants," Wilhelm said. "Which reminds me, we were able to get you tickets to a couple of shows."

Colby grinned. "And somebody to go with?"

Both men chuckled, looking at each other. He knew what they were thinking—that he was a rustic, bow-legged oaf, which was precisely what he intended. "We might be able to help out in that regard, as well," Tom Harris said.

Colby dismissed the comment with a wave of the hand. "No need for you boys to go to any trouble. Fact is, I usually manage pretty well on my own."

"I'm sure you do, Mr. Sommers."

"Colby," he said. "If we're going to be partners, no reason not to be friendly."

They laughed. There was another minute of talk about the weather. Colby continued playing dumb like a fox, always surprised how well it worked with East-erners. The thicker his accent, the more complacent they seemed to get.

When Ed Wilhelm determined that there'd been enough rapport-building, he switched into the negoti-ating mode. "Let me update you on our situation in the Edwards Plateau country. There've been develop-ments since our last conversation."

"To the good, I hope."

"Yes, we think so."

"Shoot."

"We've brought in an offshore partner and have aggressively gone after drilling rights throughout the plateau area. Tom has managed to patch together roughly thirty-seven thousand acres, all of which are under contract."

Harris unrolled a map and the three of them studied it.

"The tracts we have under lease are marked in red," Wilhelm said. "As you can see, the Gibson holdings—as we refer to the rights you control—are sitting just about in the middle of the field. Obviously, the eight thousand acres you own are important to our plans. We estimate between fifty and seventy-five million barrels of oil are involved. I won't say the tract is essential, but it's very important."

"I take it there are implications," Colby drawled.

"There are indeed." The oil executive turned to his associate. "Tom, why don't you present our revised offer?"

The younger man removed a sheet of paper from the folder on the table before him. "Colby, the bottom line is we're offering four million for drilling rights against future royalties."

"Four million." He tried not to show his shock.

"That's right."

"You boys must be pretty sure of what's in the ground."

"We are."

"You say four million against royalties. What kind of rate are we talking?"

Harris put the sheet of paper in front of Colby. "We can't be absolutely sure of the size of the reserve, of course, but if we take a moderately conservative estimate of, say, sixty million barrels, and an average price of, say, seventeen dollars per barrel, that would put the gross lease value at one billion, twenty million dollars."

"And my cut would be?"

"Just over eight million, Colby."

"At what rate?"

"That's using an owner decimal of point zero, zero eight."

Colby pondered Harris's calculation. "I expect it'd be a mite higher at point zero, zero nine, now, wouldn't it, Tom?"

The man smiled. "Yes, not quite ten percent higher."

Colby thought for a moment. "If my arithmetic is right, that'd be the better part of a million bucks."

"True."

Colby grinned. "Fellas, I kind of like the sound of point zero, zero nine."

"We can take a look at that," Ed Wilhelm said. "But, as I recall, you have some ownership issues that need to be cleared up."

"There've been developments in that regard as late as this morning," Colby said. "It appears that the co-owner of the Gibson rights is prepared to sell out to me."

"Pending our agreement?"

"Nope. She's given me her price."

"Without knowing what we're prepared to pay?"

"Let's just say the lady is eager to close the deal."

Wilhelm shrugged his shoulders. "I suppose if

you're both satisfied, that's all that matters. From our standpoint, dealing with a single individual is easier." He drummed a pencil on the table. "When will you have control of the property?"

"In a matter of days. Maybe as easily as next week."

"We're certainly ready to enter an agreement."

"And hand me a check for four million?"

"At close of escrow, yes."

Colby shook his head as he gazed out at the skyline of New York. Based on his experience on the production side, and talk he'd heard over the years, he'd expected an advance of maybe half a million dollars, which would have meant a quarter of a million for his share. Suddenly they were talking two million for a half interest and, if Liz quitclaimed her share, he could be putting a cool four million in the bank! Incredible.

"Mr. Gibson was very shrewd to have accumulated all those mineral rights," Ed Wilhelm said. "You're definitely going to benefit from his foresight."

"I don't know if this is what ol' Virgil had in mind, but I sure am in his debt."

"Did he have an inkling there was oil on the plateau?" Harris asked.

"Virgil always said the ground wasn't much good, so the value had to be what was under it. Every time he sold a few dozen acres of dirt, he'd turn around and buy mineral rights from his neighbors. Eight years ago, he swapped his grazing rights up on the bluffs straight across for two thousand acres of mineral rights. George Mueller's grandkids must be cursin' ol' Granddad about now."

"You're a very fortunate man, Colby."

"Seems that way."

"Do you have any questions?" Harris asked.

Colby thought for a minute, then said, "No, but you boys give some thought to zero, zero nine. I like the ring of it."

Both men laughed. "Tell you what," Ed Wilhelm said. "If you have clear title, and are prepared to sign a lease by the middle of next week, then you've got your zero, zero nine."

Colby nodded with satisfaction. "Sounds fair enough. Give me a specific day. I work best under deadlines."

"How about Wednesday the nineteenth at noon?"

"You boys don't like lettin' the grass grow under your feet, do you?"

"I'll be honest with you," Wilhelm said. "Our offshore partners want to move quickly."

"Guess I better talk to my gal, then. Pronto."

He got to his feet. The others did, as well. They shook hands.

"I'll be in touch," Colby told them.

"The ball's in your court."

"Yes, sir, I appreciate that fact. Wednesday, noon."

Tom Harris walked with Colby to the reception area. The receptionist greeted him with a smile.

"Would you like your coat, Mr. Sommers?"

"If it's not too much trouble, darlin'."

She went to the closet and got his sheepskin coat. Beaming, she helped him on with it. The notion of inviting her to lunch went through his mind. After all, he'd just become a millionaire. That ought to be enough to entice a pretty woman to join him for a celebration—assuming his down-home charm wasn't sufficient.

Colby was about to open his mouth with the offer, when he decided the one he really ought to be having lunch with was Liz. She was a much more practical choice. He already knew his charm wouldn't be sufficient to entice her. His newfound wealth might not be sufficient, either. But the fact remained, he needed her signature. Until then, like it or not, they were joined at the hip and neither would be going anyplace without the other.

Saying goodbye, Colby headed for the exit. He considered a plan to get inside Liz's door. She'd been adamant about him staying out of her life, so it wouldn't be easy. On the other hand, he had chips to play with. The only question was, did he share the wealth?

Waiting at the bank of elevators, Colby made a decision. He'd follow Liz's lead. If she treated him with a little common decency, she'd be two million bucks richer. If not, she'd have to make do with her memories of last night.

LIZ WAS AT HER DESK, looking over the file Frank Berkowski had left for her, when the phone rang. She
picked up the receiver.

"Moira's on line two," Westley told her.

"Thanks." She pushed the flashing button. "Hi,
kiddo, how's the hangover?"

"About a seven. How's yours?"

"I haven't had time to rate it, to be honest."

"Then how was Colby? Might as well get to the bottom line."

"Ugh."

"That bad?"

"No comment."

"Oh, that good!" Moira said.

Liz drew a deep breath, then slowly let it out. She'd
decided to keep last night's events in the closet where
they belonged, but hearing Moira's voice, she had an
overwhelming urge to bare her soul. Moira McKenzie
was the one person in the world she could tell just
about anything and be okay about it. Certain things she
could talk about with her mother, but Margaret Cabot
had a tendency to be judgmental. When *affaires du coeur*
were at issue, Liz turned to her friends, especially
Moira.

"Hang on a second," Liz said. She got up and closed

her office door, then returned to her desk. "You might as well know, we spent the night together."

There was a silence on the line. "Oh...really."

"Yes, really."

"Was the 'ugh' a comment on him or on you, Liz?"

"Me. Colby was just fine...if you define being fabulous in the sack as fine."

"Oh, poor baby. You have my sympathy."

"Actually it's not funny."

"Oh. I take it we're suffering the throes of conscience."

"That would be one way to put it."

"Your problem now is Grayson."

"Exactly."

"You going to tell him, or suffer in silence the rest of your life?"

"Frankly, I don't know what's right. Most men you wouldn't tell, but Grayson's awfully mature. And reasonable."

"Interesting characterization."

"Am I wrong?"

"You know him best," Moira said.

"What would *you* do?"

"That's a toughy."

"I'm inclined to tell him, but not right away."

"Plan to wait until after the wedding, eh?"

"You're not being very sympathetic," Liz chided. "I've just made one of the biggest mistakes of my life and my best friend is ready to take it to 'Geraldo.'"

"Sorry."

"Actually, the whole thing is stupid. I'm not sure whether to feel guilty or just embarrassed."

"It sounds like the evening had some redeeming

value. Maybe you're wrong to take it so seriously. Having a fling may be good for your soul."

"God, Moira, you sound like Wendy."

"Do you think Grayson would be suffering now if it had been him who'd had a last hurrah before the onset of marital bliss?"

"Grayson wouldn't have done it."

"What makes you so sure?"

"He knows I'd have killed him."

Moira laughed.

"Well, not for that reason, but he wouldn't have had a fling with some old girlfriend. He's far too level-headed for that."

"And you aren't?"

Liz thought about that for a moment. "Moira, I don't know what I am. The only thing I can say for sure is that when I saw Colby, I lost my head. That man has some sort of hold on me I can't explain."

"Maybe that's something that needs to be explored."

"No, it's just raw lust, weakness of the flesh. I'm fine once he's out of sight."

"Somehow that doesn't sound like you. Ariel or Wendy, maybe, even Angela, but not you."

"I know. That's *not* me!"

"I'm wondering if maybe you're overlooking something, a subconscious motive, I mean."

"Like what? A death wish?"

"I'm not sure I'd phrase it that way," Moira said with a laugh. "It might have more to do with Grayson than with Colby."

"You mean I'm trying to sabotage my engagement?"

"For example."

"Moira, that's absurd. If I didn't want to marry

Grayson, I wouldn't. I don't need to jump in bed with my ex to convince myself."

"Just a thought."

"I appreciate the input, but I see now this is something I'm just going to have to deal with on my own." She paused. "Now that I think about it, maybe I did have a subconscious motive."

"What?"

"Maybe I wanted to test my feelings for Grayson, see how hard I'd fight to keep him."

"I hate to say this, Liz, but that sounds like the sort of rationalization a man would come up with. 'I love you, honey, but I had to sleep with that woman to prove it to myself.'"

Liz laughed. "You're right."

"Hell, I think you're making too much of it. You slipped, that's all. Chalk it up to a learning experience."

"I already have. I know not to ever be around Colby Sommers again."

There was a knock on her door just then.

"Hang on, Moira. Yes, come in," she called out.

The door opened and Westley stood there, beaming, a huge bouquet of long-stem red roses in his arms. There must have been three dozen buds.

"This just arrived for you, boss," he said. "Want me to put them in a vase?"

"Please."

Westley, a slight young man with a boyish face and the puckish manner of a much younger brother, winked. "This must be your lucky day."

She wasn't sure about that. In the past, Valentine's Day had been decidedly mixed on the fortune scale.

Westley was gone before Liz remembered to ask if there was a card. She shrugged and returned to her telephone call.

"I just got three dozen red roses."

"Oh, wow! From Grayson?"

"I assume so. Who else?"

"I can think of at least one other candidate."

"Oh, God, don't even say that, Moira."

"Isn't there a card?"

"Probably out on Westley's desk."

"Go check, I'm dying to know."

Liz wasn't sure she was. It was unlikely Colby would send her flowers after the stern lecture she'd given him. And yet... "Don't you have something better to do?" Liz said. "The stock market must have gone up or down ten points while we've been gossiping."

"All right, I can take a hint. But do let me know. I'll be agonizing over it through all my Friday-night reruns."

"They're from Grayson," Liz said reassuringly.

"Unless I hear otherwise."

"I swear, Moira, you need some romance in your life."

"Tell me about it."

"Go buy some stock or something."

Moira laughed. "All right. Have a happy birthday and enjoy your evening with Grayson."

"Thanks."

"Talk to you later."

Liz hung up. For a while she sat wondering about Colby, whether he was ignoring her wishes and pursuing her despite her plea. Last time she'd sent him away, he'd accepted it, consoling himself with the money her stepfather had offered. The interest in the ranch he'd be getting this time wasn't a bad consolation prize, so if he followed the pattern he wouldn't press things. Besides, Colby had pride. If there was anything about him she didn't doubt, it was that. No, the roses had to be from Grayson.

Liz perused the file, reading Frank's notes from the meeting she'd missed that morning, when there was another knock on her door. "Come in."

It was Westley with the roses. He entered, putting the vase on the corner of her desk, then stepped back to admire the flowers.

"I was lucky to find a vase large enough. Had to borrow one."

"Did they come with a card or do I have a secret admirer?" Liz asked.

"Oh, yes. I forgot." Westley went back into the outer office and returned a moment later with a small envelope. He handed it over ceremoniously. "Anything else, madam?"

"No, you can return to your computer. At least one of us should be getting something done."

He smiled and left. No sooner had he gone when Grayson entered the outer office. Liz could tell because she heard his voice, accented with the flavor of New England. He was asking Westley whether she was in.

"Hard at work," her assistant said in reply.

Liz turned as red as the roses on her desk and looked down at the unopened envelope. She felt her stomach clench, though she couldn't say precisely why. Somehow she wasn't yet prepared to face Grayson. When he appeared at her door, she knew she had no choice but to deal with him.

Grayson Bartholomew wasn't quite as tall as Colby, and he was much slighter. He had a narrow, aristocratic face and even features. His eyes and hair were medium brown, and he exuded good breeding, though there was nothing haughty about him. When she'd first joined the firm she had thought that Grayson was a bit cold, though once she'd gotten to know him, he seemed warmer.

Still, they had only been friends and colleagues until the previous summer. One of the partners owned a summer place in the Hamptons and he'd invited all the attorneys to a Labor Day party. She and Grayson had discovered a mutual love for theater and ballet and had begun dating. She'd invited him to Thanksgiving at her parents' place in Connecticut; and he'd returned the favor by having her meet his mother over Christmas.

In the New Year, they'd begun talking about marriage. It had seemed so logical. They both loved law, had similar interests and their family backgrounds were also similar. In a way, both she and Grayson had grown up in a sheltered environment. But she'd gotten a taste of the gritty side of life with Colby. New Orleans, though only a brief interlude, had shown her things Grayson would probably never experience.

"Well, well," he said, "have you given up the law for the florist business, or do you have a secret admirer?"

Liz searched his face to see if he was kidding, but as usual his inner thoughts were unfathomable. "Aren't they from you?" she asked uncertainly.

Grayson shook his head. "I put in an order, but they're to be delivered to your apartment this evening. Not so ostentatious as these, I admit." He stepped to the desk and sniffed one of the taller buds. "You really don't know who they're from?"

Liz shook her head. "They just arrived and I haven't opened the card yet."

"Let's end the suspense, by all means."

She opened her desk drawer and removed the Waterford letter opener her mother had given her for Christmas.

"Unless you'd like me to step out," Grayson said. "Wouldn't want to intrude on a private moment."

He'd said it in a jocular way, so she knew he was kidding. In the time Liz had known him, Grayson had almost never shown signs of jealousy. Moira said it was because he was so sure of himself he'd never think there would be reason to be jealous. Liz had certainly given him no cause for doubt...that is until last night, though of course he didn't know about that.

"I have no secrets," she said, without thinking. The words bounced back, hitting her like a slap in the face. "Anyway, none that..." Caught between truth and a lie, she faltered. "None that you'd care about."

Grayson gave her one of his vaguely wicked smiles. "How can you be so sure? The enigmas in your life are intriguing to me by definition, Liz."

He was teasing her, which came as a relief. She opened the envelope and nervously pulled out the card. It simply said, "In memoriam" and was unsigned. She flushed. It had to be from Colby. But what did it mean? Was he tweaking her? Gloating? Apologizing? Thumbing his nose?

Grayson shifted his weight, sort of peeking around the flowers, but trying not to be too obvious. She looked up at him innocently. "I guess I do have a secret admirer."

"Oh?"

"It's unsigned." She handed him the card.

Grayson read the inscription. "Curious," he said, and handed it back. "No idea who?"

She shook her head, though she had a strong impulse to blurt out the truth.

"Is this a clue?" Grayson asked.

"If so, I don't know what it means." It wasn't completely untrue.

Liz agonized, knowing this was an opportunity to put her inner life in harmony with her outer one. Still, she vacillated a moment or two before plunging headlong into the truth. "Now—now that I think about it, they must be from Colby," she stammered.

"Colby." He tested the name in his memory. "Oh, your Texan."

"He's hardly mine, Grayson."

"You were once married."

"I remember."

Grayson examined the flowers as though the solution to the mystery was somehow contained in them. "He's due next week, isn't he?"

"Yes, but he came early. I ran into him at the Clairbourne last night."

"Really?"

"Chance encounter," she said, her emotional footing starting to feel shaky. "I was with Moira."

She meant the last to be reassuring, but Grayson didn't seem in the least suspicious. It probably never would occur to him to doubt her fidelity, which only made it worse. For some reason, it annoyed her that he was so oblivious.

"'In memoriam,'" Grayson said, repeating the words in the message. "Could he be referring to a death, perhaps? Or is it just his quirky personality?"

"Today would have been our tenth anniversary."

"Ah," he said as though that explained it. Then he seemed to realize it still didn't compute. "Odd thing to acknowledge. The way you've described him, Colby doesn't seem the sentimental type."

"He could be, in his way," Liz said, realizing she was not liking the drift of the conversation. This was not the time or place to come clean, so she'd been foolish to have brought it up. Better to have left it as a gift from a secret admirer.

"Wait, I think I understand what's going on," Grayson said.

Liz had a sudden sinking feeling. She held her breath.

"The man is trying to soften you up for the negotiations," Grayson explained. "He probably figures that, being a woman, you're easily manipulated. Cowboys are supposed to be pretty sexist, aren't they?"

"Somehow I don't think that's it, Grayson."

"Don't be too sure. Simple minds favor simple solutions."

"Colby didn't finish college, but he's not a dimwit," she protested. But then she wondered why she was defending Colby, of all people.

"There's got to be an explanation."

It suddenly occurred to her to follow the course of least resistance. "Maybe you're right," she said, changing tacts. "So much water has flowed under the bridge since I knew him, I can't possibly understand how he thinks now."

"I would hope not. What were you when you married him? Seventeen?"

"Eighteen."

Grayson nodded, knowingly. "He thinks he's setting you up. It's perfectly obvious, Liz. Excessive act of chivalry. I bet he was overly solicitous last night. Fawning. Probably flirted with you, thinking he could charm you into submission."

She felt her color rise and prayed Grayson wouldn't notice. But he was too preoccupied with his own analysis of the situation to take note.

"Am I right?"

"I guess you could say he was friendly," she said, her insides aching. "But not really blatant."

"He's probably a little smarter than we think. Did he tell you what sort of deal he had in mind?" Grayson asked. "Throw out any numbers?"

Liz was dying. Colby was the last person on earth she wanted to discuss. Why had she even mentioned his name? Maybe she *did* have a death wish!

"We hardly talked business at all," she said, pulling herself together. "Colby only made a passing reference to the property."

"He's clever. That's becoming obvious. He plays it cool, then sends you the flowers."

Liz wished Grayson would stop. Why did he have to be so naive? "I have no desire whatsoever to deal with Colby," she said firmly.

"Well, then, why not let me handle it for you? Probably the quickest way to bring Mr. Sommers back down to earth. I'm hardly an expert on Texans, but my understanding is the way to deal with them is man to man. They don't take women seriously, and that's probably the problem here."

"Grayson," she said, losing her patience. "I told Colby he could have the damned property. I don't want it. His attorney is going to send me a quitclaim deed."

"Isn't it worth anything?"

"I have no idea. I don't care. As far as I'm concerned, the matter's closed."

"Then you've already made your deal."

"In effect."

Grayson looked perplexed. "If you already agreed to give him the property, why the flowers and the hoopla?" He picked up the card again and studied the cryptic message. "Odd way to say thanks for the gift."

Liz groaned, hating herself. And she wasn't feeling any too charitable toward Grayson, either. Of course he couldn't possibly know the torment he was putting her through. It was really her fault. Everything was.

"Let's just drop it," she said. "Okay?"

Grayson shrugged. "I've got to make some calls anyway," he said. "My intention was just to stick my head in the door and say hi."

Liz was relieved. "I'm glad you did."

He extended his hand and she took it. Grayson gave hers a squeeze. "I'm looking forward to tonight," he said.

"Me, too."

"Sure I can't take you out? Hate you having to cook."

"No, I don't want to fight the crowds."

He leaned over her desk, giving her a kiss on the

cheek. Then he sniffed one of the buds. "There'll be more of these waiting at home for you, though not so grandiose, I'm afraid."

"I'm not taken by grand gestures, Grayson. You know that."

His smile fell somewhere between wicked and coy. "Darling, you should have told me that before I bought your ring."

Blowing her a kiss, he left the room. For a moment or two Liz sat still, feeling almost catatonic. Then she slowly lowered her head to her desk. She wasn't sure if she wanted to laugh or cry or scream. She couldn't ever recall having her emotions pulled in so many different directions at once.

Much to her chagrin, the face that popped into her mind first wasn't Grayson's. It was Colby's. She pictured him in the doorway of the hotel bathroom with nothing on but a towel tied around his waist. The mere thought of him, the things he'd done to her, made her tremble with uncertainty. Lord, would she ever exorcise him from her thoughts? How long would he haunt her...?

"Elizabeth, what on earth are you doing?"

It was her mother's voice. Liz lifted her head to see Margaret Cabot, dressed to the nines, standing at the door.

"Mother, what are you doing here?"

Margaret, a handsome woman with fine features and a slight figure much like her daughter's, looked shocked as she took the visitor's chair across the desk. "It's your birthday. Don't you remember, I'm taking you to lunch? We've had it planned for the better part of a month."

"Oh, God. Mother, I forgot completely."

"Well." Margaret Cabot appeared most displeased. It was a look Liz had seen often on her mother's face over the years. "Have you made other plans for lunch?"

Liz shook her head. "No."

Margaret seemed relieved. "Then there's no problem, is there?"

"No, I guess not. It's just that...I haven't made... reservations."

"Silly girl. I anticipated that. I know you're busy. I've got a table for us at the Russian Tea Room."

"Uh, good."

Her mother scrutinized her closely. "Is there something wrong, dear?"

"No, Mother. Why?"

"I don't know. You look harried."

"I guess I'm tired."

"Is that why you were napping just now?"

"I wasn't napping. I was...meditating."

"Meditating?"

"Oh, never mind. It doesn't matter." She looked at the clock on her credenza. "When's our reservation?"

"You have about fifteen minutes before we have to leave, if there's something you have to do."

"Only a morning's work," Liz said, half under her breath.

"Well, a person's entitled to be a bit lax on her birthday. You work hard. Felicitations, by the way."

"Thanks, Mom."

"I didn't bring your gift with me. I thought I'd give it to you the next time you and Grayson come out to the country to see us. It's too big to carry on the train."

"That'll be nice."

Margaret looked at her closely. "Darling, is your chin chapped? Did you walk to work in the cold air instead of taking a taxi?"

"No, Mother."

"What's wrong with your face?"

Liz was beginning to lose her patience. "Whisker burns, if you must know."

"Oh," Margaret said, shrinking into her chair. Then a smile crossed her face. "Grayson's getting a bit frisky in his old age, isn't he?"

"Yeah, real frisky." Liz closed the file that was open. "Come on, Mom, let's get out of here. We can go early. I'll let you buy me a drink."

"I didn't know you drank at noon on workdays."

"Mother, if you knew how this day has gone, you'd understand."

Margaret Cabot smiled. "I trust you're going to tell me all about it."

"Probably not."

Her mother looked surprised.

"You really don't want to hear," Liz said grimly. "Trust me."

THE OFFICES of Krantz, Markham & Warren were as classy as Colby expected. The reception area was light, modern, elegant. A bold abstract oil painting hung behind the receptionist. Law offices in New York seemed either to be of the contemporary variety like this one, or the more stuffy, traditional sort with lots of wood paneling, leather chairs and English hunting scenes. This seemed more Liz's style.

"May I help you?" the girl behind the desk asked, giving him the once over.

According to the nameplate, her name was Molly. Colby returned her smile.

"The name's Colby Sommers," he said, "I wanted to see Liz Cabot."

"I'm sorry, Mr. Sommers, but Ms. Cabot is at lunch."

"Hmm. When do you expect her back?"

"I take it you don't have an appointment."

"I'm afraid not."

"Perhaps you'd like to speak with Ms. Cabot's assistant."

A couple of calls came in quick succession.

"Just a moment please, Mr. Sommers," the receptionist said, taking the phone.

Colby turned to see a tall slender man moving toward him from the doorway accessing the inner offices. His expression was questioning.

"Excuse me," he said, "but did I hear Molly say that you're Mr. Sommers, Colby Sommers?"

"Yes, that's me."

The man extended his hand, a wide grin spreading across his face. "Mr. Sommers, I'm Grayson Bartholomew."

"Lizzy's fiancé."

Grayson chuckled. "Yes. Did Liz mention me last evening?"

Colby was taken aback. He wasn't sure whether to expect a fist to come flying in his direction or, at the very least a verbal attack. But it was soon evident that it was to be neither. To his relief, Colby realized that Grayson Bartholomew was only partly informed.

"Yes, she showed me her ring," Colby said amiably. "Nice stone. Not too big and the color was good."

"Liz is a wonderful woman. I'm lucky to have her."

"You are indeed," Colby returned. He slowly turned the brim of his hat in his fingers.

"You've obviously come to see her."

"Yep. As a matter of fact, I have." Colby wasn't sure how candid about his business he could be with Grayson. There was no way of knowing if the man was friend or foe. Then it occurred to him that Grayson could hardly be any more hostile than Liz had been, and he'd at least shown a modicum of friendliness. "It's regarding her father's property in Texas," he added.

"Yes, I understand Liz has agreed to cede her interest to you."

"That's the problem, Mr. Bartholomew."

"Problem? I'd think you'd be pleased."

"I am. And I'm happy to take her quitclaim deed. But I'd feel better if Liz knew what she was giving me. I don't want her goin' around after the fact sayin' I misled her."

"What, exactly, is the problem?"

"Lizzy thinks we're talkin' nickels and dimes, but there's a whole truckload of money involved."

Grayson's mild curiosity suddenly became intense interest. "There is?"

"Yes, sir, one hell of a lot."

"And Liz doesn't know."

"She wouldn't let me explain. I think she was so intent on getting things over and done with that she wouldn't stop to hear me out. So I thought I'd best make a last stab. If she wants to reconsider, fine. Barring that, I'd like the quitclaim deed so I can make my deal with Continental American."

"You're negotiating with an oil company?"

"I have an offer in hand. A *very* substantial one."

He could see the wheels turning in Grayson's head. Colby had definitely gotten his attention.

"Listen," Grayson said, "I'd like a chance to explain all this to Liz. It seems to me you're right. She needs to hear the details before she makes a final decision. I know she's gone to lunch. I'm sure her secretary can tell us where. I don't see any harm in joining her."

"Lizzy's not real eager to see me, Grayson. Unpleasant memories from the past, and all that."

Grayson smiled and put his arm around Colby's shoulders, leading him back toward the offices. "You let me worry about that."

"I'd be much obliged."

They moved along the hallway.

"So Continental American Oil has made a substantial offer, eh?" Grayson said.

"You bet."

"Everything's relative, I suppose. What's it mean to Liz? Are we talking…what…six figures?"

"More like seven."

Colby saw Grayson gulp.

"Oh."

"You see why I want Lizzy giving it to me with her eyes open."

"Indeed I do."

"Damn decent of you to help out," Colby said.

"You're a man of great integrity," Grayson told him. "I admire that."

Colby smiled to himself. Funny how business deals could make strange bedfellows.

7

THE RUSSIAN TEA ROOM was her mother's kind of place—opulent, exotic with its pasha cushions, brocade, tassels and rich, sensuous Oriental feel. Liz enjoyed coming here with her, something they'd been doing for years. It was about the only time she went. Grayson was a classic New York and continental cuisine kind of guy, though he was willing to make occasional forays into a French eatery like Café Loup in the West Village, or Peacock Alley in the Waldorf-Astoria.

Truth be known, Grayson was a little tight when it came to money and so they rarely splurged. Liz wasn't extravagant, so mostly she didn't mind his careful ways, though occasionally she felt he overdid it. Now and then, when she'd get the impulse to "do the town," she was reluctant to say so, because that wasn't Grayson's style.

Once, during the holidays, she'd suggested they go to Lutèce—she'd even offered to pay—or to Elaine's on the Upper East Side, but Grayson had balked. He didn't like the celebrity scene and took her to La Luncheonette in Chelsea instead. Good food in an intimate, quiet atmosphere was fine, but it made her wonder if Grayson wasn't completely out of tune with her deeper passions. The next night she and Moira had gone to Elaine's and had a blast rubbing shoulders with people who acted like celebrities, even if they weren't.

Margaret Cabot handed the menu back to the waiter and removed her glasses, putting them in her alligator eyeglass case, then into her purse. Liz watched her mother's graceful, if a bit studied, movements with admiration. In her mind, her mother had always been, first and foremost, a lady. And one of the great mysteries of Liz's life had been why her mother had ever married Virgil Gibson.

Not that her father didn't have his qualities. He'd been good-looking in a rugged, down-home way. And he was not stupid. Virgil had simply lived in a different world from her mother, a world with a different set of values and priorities. They'd met at a time of national crisis and had let their emotions carry them away. Her mother had only alluded to the fact indirectly, but Liz gathered that her father had been a fairly accomplished lover in his day, as well.

"So," Margaret said in that tone that indicated it was time to talk, "what's this business about Colby Sommers?"

In the taxi on the way to the restaurant Liz had mentioned Colby had come to New York to tidy up the remaining loose ends of Virgil's estate, and that she was looking forward to putting it behind her. Margaret, who rarely spoke of Colby and had a habit of changing the subject when his name came up, hadn't commented. She'd been distracted with something else, but was now retrieving it from her memory bank, as was her way. Margaret was a woman who felt strongly that there was an appropriate time and place for everything.

Over the years her mother's tendency had frequently come up against Liz's inclination toward spontaneity. Sometimes it was a source of conflict. Some passions Margaret regarded as weakness, not virtues. Liz often wondered if her mother's failed marriage had been the reason behind her measured approach to life.

"He thinks there's oil on Dad's land and he wants to exploit it," Liz explained. "Since he can't do anything without me, he's come to New York to settle up."

"What do you plan to do?"

"I told him as far as I'm concerned, he can have it. I can't be bothered fooling around with land that's virtually worthless."

"But if there's oil..."

"Mother, by the time Dad died, he didn't have enough land left to do anything with. Oil or not, it can't be worth much. The most important thing is severing all ties with the past. Specifically, with Colby."

"I couldn't agree more," Margaret said. "To be truthful, I'd completely forgotten about your interest in Virgil's land. Colby hasn't been hounding you about it, has he?"

"No, the letter I got a few days ago was the first time he's tried to contact me. But I'd rather not talk about him, if you don't mind. The matter is closed. Colby is a thing of the past in every sense of the word."

Margaret Cabot arched a brow. "If I could have convinced you of that ten years ago, I'd have saved us both a lot of suffering."

"Please, Mother, let's not get into that."

The waiter arrived with a bottle of Entre-Deux-Mers, Margaret's favorite white Bordeaux. She had Liz taste it for her.

Liz pronounced the wine fine. It wasn't until she'd had a sip that she recalled the cause of the dull throb at her temples—the champagne she'd imbibed the previous evening.

Despite herself, Liz let her mind to return to the events in Colby's hotel room the night before, the utter licentiousness of their lovemaking. Until she noticed her mother stiffen.

"Oh my God," Margaret said, looking toward the entrance. "Is that who I think it is?"

Liz looked over her shoulder to see Colby Sommers peering about the dining room. The man behind him stepped to his side.

"And there's Grayson," Margaret exclaimed. "What on earth could they be doing together?"

Liz was too stunned to speak. She could only stare.

Finally, Grayson and Colby both spotted them. Grayson led the way to their table. There was a broad, even happy, smile on his face.

"Darling," he said coming to the table, "this is your lucky day. Colby has great news." He nodded to her mother. "Hello, Margaret. Forgive us for intruding." He paused long enough to buss her on the cheek. "But I believe you'll find it worthwhile."

There were three chairs at the table. Grayson signaled the waiter to bring a fourth, then resumed his role of host.

"Margaret, I believe you remember Colby Sommers."

"Of course," she replied with icy aloofness. "Hello, Colby."

"Ma'am."

Liz, who'd been listening, was too stunned to react,

at least yet. Meanwhile, Colby, who looked like the proverbial cat who'd swallowed the canary, acknowledged her with a nod and said, "Hi, Lizzy." She colored in response.

Grayson, busy directing the arrangement of the chairs, missed the exchange. He was completely oblivious. As the men took their seats, Liz and her mother exchanged looks of dismay. All Liz could think was that Grayson better have a damned good excuse for this or she'd kill him.

"Again, my apologies," Grayson began, addressing her and then her mother in turn, "but Colby's told me something about your father's property you have to hear, Liz."

"Uh, how did you two run into each other, anyway?" she asked, looking back and forth between them.

"I stopped by your office," Colby replied. "I know you consider our business arrangement settled, but after what I learned at Continental American this morning, I couldn't leave town without bringing their offer for mineral rights to your attention."

"And we ran into each other by chance in the reception area of the office," Grayson added. "Colby told me what he's learned and I agreed that you simply had to hear."

"Good heavens," Margaret said. "If it's so important don't keep us in suspense any longer."

"Well, Mrs. Cabot," Colby began, "the bottom line is that Liz's half interest in Virgil's holdings could be worth up to three or four million bucks, once all is said and done."

Liz, Grayson and Margaret all gasped.

Liz blinked. "Three or four *million?* How is that possible?"

"That's projected royalties," Colby replied. "Nobody knows for sure, of course, until they start pumping crude. But I can tell you this much. Continental American offered me a four-million-dollar advance for drilling rights."

"Dear God," Margaret said.

"How can the oil under a little piece of land be worth that kind of money?" Liz asked, still incredulous.

"What you don't understand is that even as Virgil was selling land, he was buying up mineral rights to surrounding properties. His holdings—or more accurately, our holdings—comprise a tract of over eight thousand acres."

"Virgil had the mineral rights to eight thousand acres of oil land?" Margaret said, flabbergasted.

"Yes, ma'am."

"This is unbelievable," Liz said.

She noticed the gleeful smile on Grayson's face. No wonder. His fiancée had been transformed from a woman with a good income and the prospect of a comfortable inheritance, to a millionaire.

"There is a small problem," Colby said, running his tongue through his cheek. "As you recall, Liz, we made a deal. You were going to quitclaim your interest in the property to me in exchange for my...well, making myself scarce. Now I'm fully prepared to live up to our agreement, but I can't in good conscience ask for a deed without satisfyin' myself that, fully informed, this is still what you want." He paused. "So, I guess I'm askin'—do we have a deal or not?"

Liz gulped. Colby had put her squarely on the horns

of a dilemma. Was her word worth the sacrifice of several million dollars? That's what it came down to.

She glanced first at Grayson, who was biting his lip, then at her mother. Seeing she was bewildered, her mother stepped forward.

"Colby, dear," Margaret said in a gently persuasive voice, "you aren't suggesting that Liz is bound by a promise to give away something whose value she was ignorant of, are you? I mean, don't contracts require that everybody understand exactly what they're agreeing to? Grayson, you're a lawyer. Aren't I right about that?"

"I don't think Colby's suggesting there's a binding agreement, Margaret," he replied. "I believe he's asking her what she wants to do now that she's aware of the value of the property."

Liz had to admire Grayson's deftness. But neither his diplomacy nor the legal realities changed the fact that she was being forced to choose between money and her integrity. Not that anyone could blame her if she changed her mind, but any way she looked at it, Colby was forcing her to look him in the eye and say that money changed things. "Relative values" was the way a college professor had framed it in a course she'd taken on ethics.

"That's a fair way to frame it," Colby said, concurring with Grayson. "I want to know how Liz feels about things now."

She could see it was time to take charge. "I'm not the only one who matters, Colby," she said deftly. "You evidently came to New York with some sort of proposal in mind. Why don't you tell me what it is *you* want?"

"I want to be fair, Lizzy. That's all."

"So do I."

"What's fair to you?" he asked.

"You're the one with the plan. I only found out what's at issue a few minutes ago."

Colby seemed to enjoy their jousting, judging by the grin that played on his mouth. And by the twinkle in his eye, she would not have put it past him to be thinking about their lovemaking. That would be so like him...reveling in the fact that he and she knew something that Grayson and her mother didn't. It couldn't be a total accident that they were having this conversation in front of her fiancé and her mother.

"The situation is clear," Colby said. "At the moment, we have four choices. First, we can deal with Continental American jointly. Second, I can buy you out. Third, you can buy me out. Or fourth, we can do nothing. I could just go back to ranching and you to practicing law."

"The last would be foolish," Grayson said.

"I tend to agree," Colby replied. "How about you, Liz?"

"I suppose there's nothing to be gained by waiting."

"The next question is, do either of us have a couple of million in their checking account to buy the other out? I must confess I don't."

"Obviously, I don't, either."

"So unless you still want to quitclaim your interest over to me, I'd say we're stuck with each other, Lizzy."

She could see how much he was enjoying this. Fate couldn't have provided him with a more perfect hand for the purpose of exacting revenge. Just hours ago she'd kissed him off unceremoniously and now here he was, sitting at a table with her in the Russian Tea Room, making her eat out of his hand—in front of Grayson and her mother, no less!

"This is neither the time nor the place for making momentous decisions," Margaret said, slipping into the breach. "I have a suggestion."

"Good, let's hear it," Colby said cheerfully.

He was humoring her, and whether Margaret realized the irony in that or not, Liz didn't know. But she did know that Colby was relishing every minute of this.

"I think that the three of you should come to Connecticut for dinner this evening," Margaret explained. "That will give you all time to think everything over. Then, in a nice, quiet, unharried atmosphere, you can consider your options."

"That's a great idea," Colby said, "a wonderful idea."

He'd said it enthusiastically, but Liz knew that hidden underneath the chipper demeanor was disdain. Her mother might have realized that, too, but seemed not to care. What did matter? Millions were at stake.

"I'm afraid Grayson and I have other plans," Liz intoned, "so that's out."

"But Liz," Grayson said gently, "don't you think—"

"I'm sure Colby understands that I'd like to spend my birthday and Valentine's Day alone with my *fiancé*, Grayson," she said, cutting him off. "Dad's property is a business matter and it can be taken care of during business hours."

"That's only partly true," her mother rejoined. "Colby is no stranger to the family and I for one feel we have some making up to do for past slights."

"Why, Mrs. Cabot, that's not true," he protested. "I've always had the utmost regard for you and for your judgment. Not to bring up a sore subject, but you were right about me and Liz being wrong for each other, you know."

Her mother actually colored.

"Yes, indeed," Colby went on. "But for an accident or two of fate, Lizzy and I would have been nothing more than ships passing in the night. And if it weren't for this property of Virgil's, a chance meeting wouldn't have gone beyond, 'Howdy, how you been? You sure do look great. Nice bein' with you again, and so long.'"

Liz shot him a look, but was powerless to do anything about his jab.

"At the time, separating you two seemed the wisest course," Margaret said, fumbling. "But I'm glad you're able to look back on things so dispassionately."

"A little humility can be a man's greatest strength, ma'am."

Liz felt sick. She was tempted to tell Colby that he could have his damned oil money; it didn't mean a thing to her. But of course, she didn't have the nerve for that, and he knew it. Which made her resent him all the more. And having to witness her mother's groveling only added insult to injury.

"Be that as it may," Margaret said, recovering, "I think a little friendly society is what's called for. If tonight's not convenient, let's do it tomorrow. That would be better anyway. Gives me more time to prepare." She turned to her future son-in-law. "Grayson, you and Liz could pick Colby up at his hotel and bring him with you to the country. Don't you think that would be nice?"

"Mother..." Liz said firmly, hoping her indignant tone would be all that was necessary.

"A wonderful idea, Margaret," Grayson said, jumping in. "We don't have anything scheduled tomorrow, do we, Liz? We've been promising your folks we'd come up to Connecticut for weeks now."

"Splendid, splendid," Margaret enthused, not giving Liz a chance to protest. She turned to Colby. "How about you, dear? Does the New England countryside sound appealing?"

"It sure does. I'm game, Mrs. Cabot. And much obliged." He gave Liz a wink. "It would be a pleasure."

Liz could have killed him right on the spot. Instead, she was reduced to a sickly smile of compliance. Now she was sorry she hadn't told Grayson whose bed she'd slept in last night. That humiliation would have at least spared her this one.

Their waiter returned with menus for Colby and Grayson.

"We need two more glasses for the wine," Margaret said. "After all, we have cause to celebrate, don't we, children? It's not every day a couple of young people are handed several million dollars to divide!"

"Hear, hear!" Grayson added enthusiastically. "I think we especially need to toast Colby for his integrity."

"I couldn't agree more," Margaret concurred.

Liz saw the little twitch at the corner of Colby's mouth. What better revenge could a man ask for—especially a man who had all but been ridden out of town on a rail the last time he'd tangled with the Cabots?

Despite her annoyance, Liz couldn't help but feel a

begrudging admiration for the man. First, he'd had her begging him to take her to bed. Now he practically owned her soul. Of course, the decision about the oil still hadn't been made. She had more latitude than Colby might think. True, she needed him—or at least his cooperation. But the reverse was also the case. The question was, to whose advantage was that?

Colby leaned toward her as Grayson and Margaret dealt with the waiter. "Nice to deal with each other so amicably," he said under his breath, "don't you think?"

"Yes, very nice," she replied through a thin smile. "But you're still a bastard."

Colby chuckled. "Sure do love it when you talk dirty." Then he gave her a wink and turned to the waiter, who was ready to take his order. "I understand the caviar's not bad here," he said.

"Yes, sir," the waiter replied, "we serve the finest Persian caviar available."

"Can I get that on a French roll?" Then he laughed, grinning. "Just kidding." He studied the menu, then said. "Bring me the caviar for starters, then I'll have whatever Lizzy ordered. I always did think she had great taste in food." He handed the menu back to the waiter and gazed at Margaret. "Must have been your influence, ma'am. Safe to say she didn't get it from her daddy."

Liz couldn't help herself. She gave him a swift sharp kick in the shins.

Colby scarcely flinched; instead he laughed. Then he turned to her and, putting his hand on hers in a friendly way, said, "I must say though, Lizzy, you've got ol' Virgil's fire."

BY THE TIME they stepped out onto Fifty-seventh Street the sky had cleared and the sun was actually shining.

"This is a good omen," Margaret said, looking up through the towering buildings, her cheeks rosy from the wine. "The sun shines on happy young people with good fortune."

To Liz's dismay, Margaret had actually looped her arm in Colby's and smiled up at him. He was beaming appreciatively, but Liz knew he was gloating. She could hardly blame him, though it disgusted her the way her mother fawned.

Earlier, in the ladies' room, she'd expressed her disapproval. "Aren't you overdoing it, Mother?" she'd said. "You've got to know Colby's laughing up his sleeve at you."

"Of course he is," Margaret replied. "I'm giving him the satisfaction he wants in exchange for what we want."

"What about your dignity?"

"Elizabeth, I'm being practical. A woman can afford to be practical for four million dollars. That boy hated me ten years ago, he hates me now. He knows I'm groveling and it's exactly what he wants. I sent him home to Texas without you ten years ago for the sake of your future. I'm welcoming him into my home now for the same reason."

"That's awfully mercenary, Mother."

"A year from now it'll seem a small price to pay. Just be glad I'm willing to do it for you. While it doesn't exactly spare you the trouble of being nice to him, it at least makes it easier."

Grayson was at the curb, looking for a taxi, while

Liz, Colby and her mother chatted. Margaret checked her watch.

"Heavens, I'll miss the early train, if I don't hurry. I can't keep Weldon waiting. Grayson, you'd better get two cabs," she called as the first taxi pulled up. "I'm going to have to go directly to the station."

"I have a client I should look in on down on Forty-second Street," he said. "Why don't we share this one, Margaret?" He turned to Liz. "Would you mind going back to the office alone, darling? Maybe you and Colby can share a taxi."

"I'll be glad to see she gets safely back to the office," Colby interjected, leaving Liz with nothing to do in response but smile.

They all exchanged quick goodbyes. Liz watched her mother kiss Colby on the cheek as Grayson did the same with her. Then Margaret and Grayson were off, their taxi disappearing in the traffic.

Colby took a deep breath of the winter air and looked up at the sky. "It is a beautiful day, Lizzy. Feel like walking?"

She looked up the street to see if there was a taxi readily available, but none was in sight. "Well, maybe for a block or two," she said, "but I've got a staff meeting to prepare for this afternoon, so I'll have to grab a cab pretty soon."

They started up the street, Liz pulling the collar of her coat up around her neck. She also wore the beret she'd had on the night before. They walked for a minute or so in silence.

"Well," she finally said, "you didn't go overboard with the gloating. I suppose I have to hand you that."

"Gloating?"

"Come on, Colby," she said, "don't give me the innocent act. You reveled in the fact that you had my mother kissing your feet."

"Actually, I felt a little sorry for her."

Liz saw that he was sincere. It occurred to her that that said a lot about him.

"She felt she was sacrificing for me."

"Not knowing we'd already kissed and made up."

Liz gave him a look. "I knew you wouldn't be able to resist throwing that in my face."

"I didn't mean it snidely, Liz. To the contrary, I meant it with great affection. Waking up this morning with you in my bed has been the high point of my day, sugar. By the way, did you get my flowers?"

"Yes. What was the point of that? I thought we had an agreement you'd stay out of my life?"

"Oh, so the quitclaim deed deal is back on, eh?"

She shot him a wicked glare.

He chuckled.

An ambulance passed, its siren blaring. For a time they couldn't speak because of the din. Finally it disappeared up the street.

Colby turned to her and said, "Actually, I sent the flowers to prepare you for this reunion. I knew you wouldn't want me to skip town without letting you know what you were giving away."

"Why didn't you just have your attorney send me the quitclaim deed? I had every intention of signing it, you know."

"I'm aware of that, but I also know you'd have had recourse against me. You could have alleged fraud or whatever. No court would have agreed you intended to give away two million bucks for essentially nothing. Let's just say I decided to save myself the trouble of a lawsuit."

"That's all? That's the only reason for the flowers and the visit?"

"I had no idea I'd be seeing your mother today."

"That's not what I meant."

"Then what are you getting at?"

She gave him a knowing smile. "Maybe *I'm* gloating."

Colby put his arm around her shoulders in a friendly way. "After last night, I won't deny that seeing you is a pleasure. But you have to admit I have a pretty good excuse."

They approached a grizzled old panhandler sitting on a heating grate and moved to the side to pass him.

"Hey, buddy," the man called to Colby, "it's Valentine's Day. How about a little love for me?"

Colby stopped, fished under his sheepskin coat for his wallet and handed the man a ten-dollar bill. The panhandler's eyes lit up.

"Wow, love you, man!" He kissed the bill. "Hope he was as good to you, lady."

Liz and Colby went on, both smiling.

"Glad you didn't tell him you got two million," Colby said. "I might have had a friend for life."

Liz reflected on the comment. "I hope you don't think the money has fundamentally changed anything," she said.

"At least we're talking. That's something."

They came to a corner and stopped, waiting for the

light to change. Liz looked up at him, her eyes watery from the cold. A cacophony of automobile horns echoed up the canyon of Avenue of the Americas from the direction of Central Park.

"Colby, I want you to know I meant every word I said this morning."

"You're saying you want me to beg off dinner at your mother's tomorrow night."

"No. Maybe you're entitled to the satisfaction of seeing my mother twist in the wind. You've certainly gotten the last laugh with me, so I'll let you have another moment of revenge. But I've got to be honest with you about my feelings."

The light changed and they started across the street.

"I understand where you're coming from," he said. "You've made your feelings clear. But I don't want you to misunderstand what happened last night. That was not revenge in any sense of the word. I enjoyed being with you."

They'd come to the other side of the street. Liz stopped, facing him as pedestrians hurried past. Her eyes shimmered even more, as much from emotion as the cold air.

"I love Grayson and I'm going to marry him," she said. "That makes everything else irrelevant."

Colby peered deeply into her eyes. "Damned strange conversation to be having on our tenth anniversary, isn't it, Lizzy?"

She bit her lip, feeling the tears begin to well. Glancing at the street, she saw a cab stopped at the light. It was available.

Without a word, she ran and jumped into the back seat. The light changed and the taxi took off. Liz did not look back. She did not want to see Colby's face.

8

LIZ HAD TAKEN only a few bites of her dinner, though Grayson had pronounced his fillet wonderful. He'd eaten everything—the asparagus topped with béarnaise sauce, the baked potato and sour cream—and still fully informed her of his conversation that afternoon with Ed Wilhelm over at Continental American. Grayson had grown more and more excited as he'd waxed eloquent on his expectations for the Edwards Plateau county field.

She had listened, wanting to share his enthusiasm. Of course she was happy—a little overwhelmed, actually—but somehow she had trouble matching his mood. Even the dozen short-stemmed roses, sitting on her sideboard from Grayson hadn't cheered her. Instead, during dinner she'd spent her time staring past him at Colby's roses in the front room. She'd brought them home with her, wrapped in newspaper, knowing they'd be wasted at the office over the weekend.

The cabbie had asked if she was a flower wholesaler. His brother-in-law in Jersey was a florist. Liz had given the man a rosebud when she handed him the tip.

"Have a nice Valentine's Day," he'd said. "Pretty lady like you shouldn't have any trouble."

She'd told Grayson the story and he'd said if he lived in New York a hundred years he still wouldn't get used to cabbies. He recounted how he liked his cabbies and his waiters mute, the way God and good manners intended it.

"So what are you going to do with the first two mil?" Grayson asked after she'd let the conversation lapse."

"Pardon?"

"The money. Given any thought to what you'll do with it?"

"Oh, no, not really. I'll invest most of it, I suppose. And I'll give some away. To a home for troubled teenagers in Texas, or something like that."

Grayson looked perplexed. "Is there a particular one you have in mind?"

"No, but there must be one. I think I'd make the donation in my father's name. Build a recreation hall or something."

"Sounds like you have given it some thought."

"No, that just came off the top of my head. I don't even know why I said it."

"Charitable impulse maybe."

"Yes, that must be it."

A terrible, desperate feeling suddenly came over her. Liz had an urge to jump up from the table. She didn't even know why. All afternoon, she'd been irritable. Frank Berkowski, the partner she worked for and one of the few people at the office she'd told about the inheritance, had congratulated her and asked if she was going to retire. Liz hadn't even laughed. "That's the last thing I'd do, Frank," she told him. "I refuse to let this money change my life."

It wasn't until she saw the surprised look on Frank's face that she realized she'd been defensive about it, even though she should have known he was kidding. She'd apologized then, saying the day's events had given her a case of the nerves. That wasn't characteristic of her, not "Iron Liz" as some of the associates called her. Frank, an affable man of considerable girth and a fine attorney, brushed it aside.

Liz had not wanted to be unprofessional, so she'd pulled herself together enough to give Frank her reaction to what had come up in the morning's meeting. After their discussion she'd agreed to draft a revision in the interrogatories she and Alex had prepared the week before.

"Maybe you should take a few days off, Liz," Frank had told her as he was about to leave. "Sometimes it's good to let big events like this settle a bit. Helps to gain perspective."

"Thanks," she'd told him, "but I'm fine. Grayson and I are driving up to see my parents over the weekend. A good long walk in the snowy countryside is all I need."

"Take your long johns," Frank said, his hand on the doorknob. "We're scheduled to get a huge storm this weekend, you know."

"I didn't know."

"It's supposed to put the flurries we've been having recently to shame."

"Well, I can handle it. I grew up in Connecticut, don't forget."

"Then make sure Grayson takes his woollies."

Frank Berkowski was a decent fellow, twenty years older than she—almost, but not quite, of her dad's generation. Over the holidays, when it began to look like Grayson would propose, she'd asked Frank what kind of impact he thought marriage would have on her career. "It's not required, and I'd certainly hate losing you, but in the long run, you'd probably be better off in a different firm," he'd replied. "Unless you could convince Grayson to leave, which, from my point of view, would be the best of all worlds."

Frank and Grayson were not close, but being partners, they'd gotten along well enough. Yet, Liz had always sensed that Frank didn't approve of her relationship with Grayson, though more for personal than professional reasons. Frank's wife, Gladys, was a lawyer and had a family law practice on Long Island. "Limit your talk about work to the hour before dinner," Gladys had advised. "It's the only way for two lawyers to keep any semblance of a sane marriage."

The comment had haunted Liz all afternoon. She kept asking herself if she really wanted to talk to Grayson about law every night of her life before they sat down to their cutlet, or fillet of sole, or chicken. In contrast, she kept picturing the run-down residential hotel in New Orleans where she and Colby sat under a naked light bulb, eating cheeseburgers and trying to figure out where they were going to get the money for their next meal.

It had been a miserable existence, yet at the same time so vibrant and elemental. Sitting at her desk that afternoon, Liz had pondered how they'd have reacted if somebody had knocked on their door back then and told them they'd each get two million dollars. It would have seemed a fairy tale come true.

They'd have bought land and stock so that Colby could ranch. And Liz would have gone on to college. They'd talked about that, anyway. Colby had told her he wanted to go back to A&M to finish his degree, too. That had been part of his dream.

They'd often talked about the way they would live once they made it. They'd have kids. Liz would read Emily Dickinson's poems to their children, and Colby would teach them to ride. "And I'll read Robert Frost poems to them by the fire in the evenings," he'd said.

She'd remembered the conversation clearly. It had taken place in Audubon Park in New Orleans, under a big old shade tree. They'd split a lemonade and Liz sat sipping on the straw, listening to Colby telling her his dreams, his head in her lap, looking up at the new spring leaves over their heads.

"Why Robert Frost?" she asked.

"Because he's the only poet I've ever read," he admitted with a laugh.

Nobody could ever mention poetry without her thinking about that conversation, that day. It was one of the offbeat little things about him that had stuck with her.

"Liz? You all right? You seem distracted."

She snapped out of her reverie, realizing she'd been daydreaming. Grayson seemed more concerned than offended.

"Sorry," she said, "my mind was wandering. I'm not myself today."

"Must be all the excitement." He looked at her plate. "Aren't you going to have any of the wonderful dinner you made?"

She sighed. "Oh, no, I'm not hungry. But don't worry, I'll wrap it up and have it for lunch."

"Will you have a piece of that birthday cake I brought?" Grayson asked.

Liz had forgotten about him showing up at the door with a cake box and the "Happy Birthday" on his lips.

She'd been touched, which of course made her feel guilty because she hadn't had very charitable thoughts about him. In truth, she'd resented the fact that money had reared its ugly head. Of course, Grayson couldn't be accused of being mercenary, because he'd asked her to marry him before he knew about the oil money. And yet, he seemed too...something. Too happy, maybe. If that was possible.

"Liz?"

"Huh?"

"Birthday cake?"

"Oh, yeah. As long as you don't put twenty-eight candles on it."

Grayson laughed and got to his feet. Liz started to get up, as well, but he told her to stay seated. "You're the birthday girl."

"At least let me clear the table."

"No. Not on your birthday."

"But it's Valentine's Day, too. And that's a day for both of us."

He gave her his broad smile. "It's more your day."

She sat back in her chair, returning to her musing as Grayson cleared the table. As he was on his way to the kitchen for the last time, she called to him. "Grayson."

He turned. "Yes, darling?"

"Please don't take this wrong, but would it be all right if you didn't spend the night?"

He was momentarily taken aback. "Well...sure." Then, frowning, "But is something wrong, Liz?"

"No, it's just that I'm not feeling myself. I've had this terrible headache all day and...well, I just don't feel like I'd be good company."

"You know you're always good company, Liz, no matter what."

"That's sweet of you to say, but I don't feel like I'm much fun."

"Other than being distracted, you seem fine to me."

"I've tried not to be a party pooper."

"Well, I just want you to be happy, darling. If you're not well, I can leave after we have our cake and coffee."

"I don't mean for you to run off," she said, feeling guilty.

"Don't worry. You just relax. While I get the cake, you can start thinking of a birthday wish."

Liz smiled as he left the room. Grayson was so nice. She hated herself for having selfish, disloyal thoughts. The fact of the matter was, her headache had been pretty well gone by noon. And she'd had next to no wine at lunch.

If there was a problem, it was more emotional than physical. She simply didn't want to sleep with Grayson and she wasn't sure why. The only reason that came to mind was that it would amplify the guilt she was already feeling about her fling with Colby.

Liz asked herself it she needed to tell Grayson everything that had happened the night before, but decided she couldn't. It would just make tomorrow impossible.

She'd also flirted with the idea of calling Colby and asking him to beg off. There was nothing to be gained by him going to Connecticut. He'd already had his fun at her expense, and her mother's.

Thank God he hadn't tried to meddle in her relationship with Grayson. It would have been easy enough for him to throw in a zinger or two, nettle Grayson about the past. If he'd wanted to be troublesome, he could have found a way to bring up last night, but fortunately he was an honorable person. Colby could be a bastard, but he did have a sense of propriety.

Grayson returned then, carrying the cake. A single candle was stuck in the middle. When he set it down on the table, Liz saw that the cake was heart shaped. Her guilty thoughts, the sweetness of Grayson's act, the emotion of the day, everything caught up with her at once. Her eyes flooded.

"Have you thought of a wish?" he asked.

The first thought that came to mind was that she wanted Colby to hurry up and get out of her life. He'd put a crack in her relationship with Grayson and her fiancé wasn't even aware of it.

She drew an unsteady breath. "Yes, I think so."

"Well, here's your chance to make it come true."

Liz looked up at him and they exchanged smiles. She took his hand, perhaps for reassurance, then turned her attention to the wobbling flame.

Suddenly another dusky moment from the past flashed into her mind. She was with Colby in their room in New Orleans; a single cupcake with a burning candle stuck in it sat on a wooden chair between them. The day was March 14, the one-month anniversary of their marriage. "We'll have better celebrations down the line, sugar," he'd said. "I promise you."

Liz, unable to help herself that night, had started crying. She hadn't been able to blow out the candle. Colby had had to do it alone.

Staring at the flame before her now, her eyes filled and the next thing she knew, tears were running down her cheeks. Her breath wedged in her throat and she could scarcely breathe, let alone blow.

"Darling?" Grayson said, his voice registering concern.

"Will you blow it out for me?" she asked in a small voice, barely able to keep from sobbing.

Grayson leaned over and blew out the candle. Liz got to her feet and turned in to his embrace. She didn't know what was wrong with her. She was just never this way. Not since she was a kid, anyway.

Grayson rubbed her back. "Poor thing. You've had a big day, Lizzy."

She stiffened, immediately pulling back. "Grayson, don't call me Lizzy. Ever."

He was shocked by her adamant tone. "Sorry, darling."

"Why did you call me that?"

"Well...I...guess from hearing Colby. It seemed endearing. And your mother...I've heard her call you Lizzy on occasion, too."

"Colby's the reason I don't like the name. Please, call me Liz. Or Elizabeth, if you have to. My mother calls me Elizabeth sometimes."

Grayson put his hand to her cheek. "You poor thing. Not feeling well and I go and blunder on top of everything else."

Liz took a steadying breath and rubbed her forehead. "I don't know what's wrong with me, Grayson. I'm sorry I jumped at you. That was unnecessary."

"At least I know not to call you Lizzy anymore," he said with a laugh. He motioned for her to sit. "Come now, cut the cake." Then he reached into his pocket and set a small ring-size box next to her place. "After you do, you can open this. It's a little birthday and Valentine's Day present."

Liz put her arms around his neck and kissed him. "You're so sweet, Grayson. I don't deserve you."

"Nonsense. Now, let's have our cake." He helped her with her chair, then returned to his place at the other end of the small table.

She took the knife, catching herself before cutting the heart-shaped cake clean in half. She wasn't sure why the impulse had struck her—unless it was because that night in New Orleans she'd cut the cupcake into two pieces. She had to will her hand to be steady. Why was she letting Colby affect her so? Couldn't she do anything without thoughts of him intruding?

Liz cut two neat pieces of cake from the bottom of the heart and put them on plates, handing one to Grayson. They looked into each other's eyes. She started to tell him that she'd changed her mind and she wanted him to spend the night, but her jaw locked and she couldn't get the words out.

Grayson picked up his fork and so did she. The words of advice from Gladys Berkowski came to mind. "You never told me about your day," she said. "Any new developments in the Smithson case?"

It was the opening Grayson needed. He loved the law. While he talked about the settlement conference that he'd attended that afternoon, Liz listened to the wind kicking up outside, rattling the window. Grayson didn't notice.

LIZ PACED BACK AND FORTH in her bedroom, weighing Grayson's Harvard class ring in her hand, along with the chain he'd given her. He told her he knew she probably wouldn't actually want to wear it, but that he'd originally gotten it with the intention of giving it to the girl he loved. The only problem was, Liz had come along a little later than he'd expected.

The sentiment had touched her, even if it was a bit corny. After he'd left she'd spent twenty minutes staring at Colby's red roses, asking herself how she was going to exorcise him from her consciousness.

Finally she'd dressed for bed, though sleep was the farthest thing from her mind. She was so nervous and distracted that she couldn't calm down. Grayson's ring, she'd hoped, might ward off tempting thoughts of Colby, but it wasn't working. She just kept staring at the telephone, knowing she wanted to call him.

Liz didn't even know what she'd say. All she knew was she wanted to make a connection with him, and let things happen from there. Maybe what she secretly wanted was for him to come to her place. If she chose to, she could make it known that she'd sent Grayson home. Would Colby wait for her to invite him to her apartment? Probably. She suspected that he wouldn't suggest it himself.

Putting Grayson's ring down on her dresser, she went and sat on the bed next to the telephone. Why was she torturing herself? Hadn't she gotten her fill of him last night?

Anyway, how could she be sure Colby would be interested? He'd enjoyed last night well enough, there was no disputing that, but maybe he'd already had what he wanted: the last laugh. For all she knew, he could be with another woman right now, somebody he'd picked up. And why not? He wasn't the type to mope over a lost love. Besides, he'd met her fiancé and she'd made it pretty damned clear to him she intended to marry Grayson.

But she did have a reason to call. They had to let Colby know what time they'd pick him up for the drive to her mother's place. She'd planned to call in the morning, but she could do it now, even if it was late. It was possible he wasn't even in, of course. For all she knew he was out painting the town red. God knew, he had good reason, considering the money he'd come in to.

Growing disgusted with her own vacillation, Liz picked up the phone and called information for the number of the Clairbourne. When the hotel operator asked her which guest she wanted to speak with, she nearly hung up, but managed to get out Colby's name. He picked up the phone on the second ring.

"Hello?" he said.

Liz's stomach clenched. She felt like a silly teenager trying to get up the nerve to ask a boy to a dance.

"Hello?" he said again.

"C-Colby?" she stammered.

"Liz, is that you?"

"Yes," she said.

"Is something wrong?"

She cleared her throat. "No, sorry. I'm fine." She cleared her throat again. "I hope I'm not calling too late."

"No, I was just watching the news."

Liz could hear the TV in the background. That made her feel better. She didn't want there to be another woman in his room. "I realized we needed to tell you what time we'd pick you up tomorrow," she said.

"Oh, yeah."

"Grayson thought we would be wise to get an early start. They say a storm's coming in."

"That's what they said on the weather."

"Would right after lunch be okay, say around one-thirty?"

"That'd be fine," he said.

"Good."

"Did Grayson say how he was dressing?" Colby asked. "I thought I'd try to fit in a little better than I did today. You see, I was in my negotiating clothes," he said with a laugh, "but tomorrow ought to be a little more relaxed and I thought I'd dress accordingly."

"Whatever you want to wear is fine."

"Could you ask Grayson?"

"If you like."

"Well, is he there?"

Liz suddenly saw what he was getting at. What's more, he'd asked the very question she'd hoped he would ask. But she wasn't sure if she wanted him to know or not. "Uh...yes," she stammered.

"Would you mind asking him, then?"

Liz's brain locked. For a woman whose profession it was to think on her feet, she was practically catatonic, afraid both to tell the truth and to lie. "What I mean is...Grayson was here...but he went home."

"Oh, I see."

"So I can't ask him."

"No, I guess you can't."

"But if you want, I can call him in the morning. My guess is he'll wear a jacket, but not a tie."

"That's all I need to know."

"Yes. Fine."

There was silence on the line. She took an unsteady

breath, feeling stupid and anxious, desperately wanting the conversation to end and not end.

"Lizzy, are you all right?" he asked with genuine concern.

"Why, yes, of course."

"You sound funny."

"How so?"

"I don't know, like somebody's got a gun to your head or something."

There was another silence. She fought the temptation to ask if he wanted to come over, pleading with herself to say goodbye.

"Oh, by the way," Colby said, "you got away so suddenly this afternoon that I didn't get to tell you something."

"What?"

"You and I can make the better part of a million extra if we sign with Continental American by Wednesday the nineteenth at noon."

"Can we do that?"

"Well, sweetheart, I guess that's kind of up to us."

Liz couldn't tell whether he'd called her "sweetheart" to be suggestive or out of habit. She closed her eyes, remembering the taste of his mouth, his strong arms around her. She was torn, so torn. And yet she knew what she had to do.

"I don't see any reason why we can't come to an agreement tomorrow," she said.

"Me neither."

Another silence.

"Colby?"

"Yes?"

"Would you want to..." Her jaw locked again.

"Would I want to what?"

"Would you rather not go up to Connecticut?" she blurted. "I can tell Mother we decided not to come because of the weather. We can do whatever we need to do in terms of an agreement here."

He hesitated. "Frankly, I sort of think your mama was lookin' forward to us coming. And to be honest, so was I."

"Oh, I see."

"If that's all right with you."

"Sure," she said. "Sure."

They both fell silent again.

"Well, I guess that takes care of things," she said, hating the conversation.

"I reckon so."

Again she fought the temptation to ask him to come over.

"Liz," Colby said, "forgive the personal question, but what in the hell is Grayson doing leaving you alone on your birthday and Valentine's Day night? Don't these city boys have a sense of romance?"

She considered saying it was because she wasn't feeling well, but chose instead to show indignation at his presumption. "You're right, it *is* a personal question. Good night, Colby. See you tomorrow afternoon." Then, without another word, she hung up.

February 15

THE STREETS OF MANHATTAN at seven o'clock on a blustery Saturday morning were busier than Colby would've thought. He'd hoped for a semblance of isolation in the concrete canyons of the city, but relative tranquillity was the best New York could offer. A solitary ride on the buttes above his ranch, it was not.

Still, it was outdoors. The air was relatively clear and the sounds of the city mute in comparison to a weekday. And it *was* exercise.

Colby had headed north on Park Avenue, leaning at times into the gusting wind, tucking his chin to keep his Stetson from flying away. Though he was not specifically going to Liz's apartment, he was headed in that direction, toward the Upper East Side. His intention was to walk for a while in Central Park, but if he could see her neighborhood along the way, why not?

Colby had awakened that morning wondering why he was not happier, now that he was a millionaire. Perhaps it was because he was not taken completely by surprise, Continental American's offer being, in effect, anticlimactic. He'd known the mineral rights were worth a lot of money, he just hadn't known it would be that much.

It was obvious his mood had little to do with the oil

deal. No, the problem was New York itself, or more specifically *Liz* and New York. Things had not worked out as he'd expected.

His feelings for Liz had developed a mind of their own. He'd started by playing games—personal more than business—and now he was stuck, thinking about her in ways that weren't productive. Plain and simple, he'd let himself get infatuated with her again.

Half an hour of walking brought him to East Sixty-ninth Street. He turned west, toward the park, and soon came to Liz's building. Stepping into the recessed entry of a building across the street where he was protected from the wind, Colby peered up at the facade of her apartment tower.

A leaden sky hung over New York, adding to the forbidding nature of the scene. He imagined Liz inside, asleep in her bed, oblivious to the fact he was passing by. He wasn't even sure why he'd come, apart from curiosity and a desire to connect with her in some vague, figurative way.

Sometimes he wondered what possessed human beings to want to live in these artificial caves, these virtual honeycombs of urban humanity. The Upper East Side was one of the more desirable neighborhoods, yet he could not imagine spending a lifetime here. There were New Yorkers who'd never gone west of the Hudson and had no desire to do so. To leave their hive was to leave life. Central Park and Coney Island were all the nature they'd ever need.

He knew that Liz was not that way. She had come to appreciate Texas and Louisiana while they were there, though she was anything but a country girl. Despite her love of the great outdoors, Liz was in her element here in New York. At Virgil's ranch, she'd been on vacation. And New Orleans had been a fleeting adventure.

They were oil and water, and yet he had a strong desire to experience her. Her engagement to Grayson only made it worse. The fact that she'd rejected him compounded his desire. And knowing she was at war with herself because of him only made it harder. He was as torn as she.

Yesterday he'd humbled her in front of Grayson and her mother. It had to have been terribly humiliating for her. And yet it had given him no real satisfaction. Somehow, having Liz beholden to him was not something he enjoyed in the least.

Colby was uncertain what he should do. Logic dictated one course, but desire another. At one level he wanted to run the string out as far as it would go. At another, he simply wanted to be done with it. He could conceive of no victory that was a true victory, except to be with her. And that was impossible.

Stepping back out onto the sidewalk, he proceeded up the street toward Central Park. Expending energy was the only thing that would help right now. Without a horse, it wouldn't be quite as satisfying. But he wouldn't have to wait long before he'd be home again. Away from the big city. Away from Liz.

LIZ HAD A CALL from Grayson at around eight-thirty. She'd been asleep, but pretended she hadn't.

"Sorry to call so early, darling," he said, "but my brother Darren just phoned with distressing news. My mother's had another stroke."

"Oh, Grayson."

"She's in the hospital in Boston. It's more serious than the last one, but the preliminary indications are that the damage isn't too severe. Darren said her speech has been affected some, but that's all they've detected so far."

"I'm so sorry."

"Needless to say, it's come at a bad time."

"Are you going to Boston?"

"I thought I would tomorrow. My brother and Julia are with her, so if I see her on Sunday, that should be good enough. I'm sure she'd like it if I flew right up, but I left Darren your parents phone number just in case."

"Oh, Grayson, dinner at Mother's isn't important. I'm not even sure it's a good idea, considering the storm that's due in. I've been thinking I ought to call Mother and cancel."

"No, to the contrary, it's very important. That fellow, Wilhelm, at Continental American would like a firm contract by the middle of next week. Business law's my field and I've talked to people about oil leases. Besides, I want very much to be of help."

"That's sweet, but it doesn't mean you have to neglect your mother, Grayson. Colby and I can negotiate the deal. We have several days."

"Yes, but Margaret was right to pave the way by giving Colby his due. It will be easier, as your mother suggests. Anyway, Colby confided to me that he was looking forward to seeing your family."

"He just wants to rub our nose in the fact that he's made good and we're indebted to him."

"That's his due, so why not accommodate him? And

I think I can be a moderating force. That's why I want to be there."

"Grayson, we're blowing this all out of proportion."

"Darling, I think Colby can be stubborn if he chooses. The man has an air of independence. He seems decent, but frankly I don't trust him to be entirely rational if he gets it in his mind there's an advantage to being headstrong."

"What are you talking about?"

"Let's just say I sense something about him," Grayson replied. "He's hiding something."

Grayson's insight, if that's what it was, surprised her. Normally he wasn't observant when it came to people. But then, maybe she'd underestimated him. "What sort of thing do you mean?"

He hesitated, and Liz was afraid he was going to make some remark about Colby having feelings for her. She waited uneasily as he hemmed and hawed.

"I don't even like bringing it up," he began, "but I wonder if your cowboy isn't setting you up for some strong-arm tactics. Maybe he hopes to squeeze a little extra out of the deal."

She was relieved to hear that was all he had in mind. "What can he do?"

"Wilhelm told me Colby was dumb as a fox."

"Maybe Mr. Wilhelm sees it to his advantage to keep us all off balance, Grayson. Believe me, I'm not worrying about Colby...pulling a fast one."

"Maybe you're a bit more susceptible to that down-home charm than you think, Liz."

She bristled. Grayson, for all his kindness, could be patronizing. "And so you feel you need to protect me."

"No, I just want to be of help. I care about you, Liz. And this is very important to our future."

She wondered if that wasn't the truest thing he'd said. It was in his interest to go with her to Connecticut, so his mother could wait until Sunday to see him. She wasn't going to throw it in his face, but it bothered her.

"If you feel it's that important, fine. Personally, I'd rather not go at all."

"Let's do the deal with Colby and then put it behind us," he said. "If you'd like, you can come to Boston with me. I'm sure Mother would love to see you."

That made her wonder if Grayson might not be jealous of Colby after all, but she wasn't going to probe to find out. "Let's see how things go," she said, giving him something to think about.

"All right, darling. Whatever you wish. Does Colby know when we're picking him up?"

"Yes, I spoke with him last night."

"Last night?"

"I called him after you left."

"Oh, I see." He paused. "Well, I guess everything is arranged then."

"Yes, I guess so."

They said goodbye and Liz hung up. For some reason the conversation annoyed her. Grayson had done nothing horrible, but he'd displeased her. She didn't like being patronized, and she didn't like the way he'd put the business deal before his mother.

Liz told herself she was just in a bad mood. Once Colby was gone, things would settle back to normal. Yes, Colby was the problem. He had upset everything. Life had been just fine until he'd shown up. She was never more sorry than now that she'd slept with him. It had been a terrible mistake.

THEY ARRIVED at the Clairbourne Hotel a little earlier than scheduled, so while Grayson waited in the car, Liz went inside to let Colby know they were there. She called his room on the house phone, but there was no answer. She hoped that he was on his way down, afraid they'd somehow gotten their signals crossed.

Liz moved toward the elevators in the hope that he'd appear momentarily. The mere sight of those brass doors reminded her of Thursday night. She had been tipsy, but not too tipsy to forget all the wonderful things Colby had done to her after they'd taken that elevator up to his room.

Just thinking about it made her flush. And worse, though she told herself she wasn't really the woman who did all those irresponsible, wild things, she felt a sudden rush of desire to do all those very same things again. Now. Right now.

If Grayson weren't outside in the car, if she'd just walked into the hotel on her own, she could easily picture herself going to Colby's room and knocking on the door, just to see what would happen.

Well, she knew what would happen—at least if it were up to her. It horrified her to think that she could be so depraved with Grayson's ring on her finger. And yet, the desire was very real.

The doors to one of the elevators opened and an attractive brunette with long, straight hair and a very short skirt exited, followed immediately by Colby. He was checking out the woman's legs and didn't see Liz until the woman passed her. It wasn't until then that she realized they weren't together.

Colby smiled at the sight of her. "Oh, you're early."

"Yes. Grayson's out front." Liz glanced back to see the brunette at the reception desk, giving her key to the clerk. She turned back to Colby. "I thought maybe you'd made a friend," she said dryly. "Pity you have plans for dinner."

Colby looked after the woman. "Doesn't matter. Monique's checking out. Has to catch a flight for Chicago this afternoon. So it's *adiós*."

Liz blinked. "Oh."

Colby broke into a broad grin, laughing. "Just kidding," he said. "Made it up. Actually, she got on a few floors below mine. Didn't have time to make her acquaintance, I'm afraid."

Liz was embarrassed to have said anything, realizing her jealousy was so obvious. "Very funny. Of course, I wouldn't have been surprised if Monique was her name and you'd had breakfast with her."

He reached out and pinched her cheek. "That almost sounded like jealousy, little lady. Or is my ego running away with me?"

"Your ego's running away with you."

Colby took his topcoat off his arm to put it on. It was only then that she realized he was dressed differently. He wore a gray tweed sport coat over a black cashmere turtleneck sweater. The combination went well with his dark hair and pale blue eyes. Looking at him, she was rather stunned. Had she ever seen him in anything other than jeans or Western wear? she wondered.

Then she remembered she had—at a dinner party he'd attended at her mother's invitation that time he'd come to reclaim her. He'd borrowed a shirt, tie and jacket from her stepfather so that he'd look halfway normal among the guests. The fit wasn't the best, but the clothes weren't as disastrous as his awkwardness. Only later did she realize the party had been a deliberate trap set by her mother to expose his weaknesses.

But Colby knew he'd been bushwhacked. And he'd been bitter that Liz had been willing to put him through such an ordeal. She'd felt sorry for him, naturally, but there'd been no avoiding the fact that he didn't belong. His humiliation opened her eyes. That evening had been a turning point in their relationship.

The impression now was completely different. Colby not only looked natural in city clothes, he looked rather sophisticated. He noticed her checking him out.

"Do you approve?"

"You look very nice," she said. "Do you often dress this way?"

"Not on the ranch, of course, but I dress like this if I'm traveling. Not to disillusion you, Liz, but everybody in Texas isn't a cowboy. There are folks there who dress this way all the time."

"I know," Liz said. "But don't forget, when I was there I did spend most of my time on the ranch. You and my dad were always in a hat and boots."

"Well, today I'm slumming."

Liz laughed.

Colby looked at his watch. "You did say Grayson was waiting."

"Oh, I forgot. And here we are gossiping."

The little smile at the corners of his mouth told her he was amused. "I won't mention that we forgot about him. Let's say I was late coming down."

"There's no need to lie. Grayson and I have a very open relationship."

"Yes. I've gotten that impression."

She could have killed him, but she refused to give him the satisfaction of knowing anything he said mattered. "How long are you going to hold that indiscretion over my head?" she asked as they headed for the entrance.

"I'm not holding it over your head, sweetheart. I just think about it every time you look into my eyes."

"You might look like a gentleman, Colby, but you aren't one."

"The important thing is we understand each other," he said, holding the door for her.

"No, the important thing is that you continue to pretend that you're a gentleman."

"Are you going to make it worth my while?" he teased.

"Yeah. If you don't, I'll kill you."

"Well," he said as they made their way toward Grayson's Lexus, "at least I know where I stand."

BY THE TIME THEY REACHED the New England Thruway in New Rochelle, it was snowing. When they got to the Connecticut state line, it was approaching blizzard conditions.

Liz, who'd opted for the back seat, to give Grayson and Colby a chance to talk, had listened to the men's sparring. They both had reason to keep things harmonious but there was a clash of egos going on all the same. Each in his own way was showing off for her.

Liz was amazed at what an astute businessman Colby appeared to be. He even knew a little about the law. He'd been picking Grayson's brain about tax considerations concerning the oil deal, and at the same time giving Grayson a primer on the oil business and ranching. One or the other of them would bring her into the conversation from time to time, but her comments were intentionally succinct. She preferred to listen.

But as driving conditions worsened, she began to worry. "I think it was a mistake to make this trip under these conditions," she said as they passed a fender bender on the side of the road.

"It makes it more exciting," Grayson replied cavalierly.

"Yeah, well, what if we can't get home?"

"It'll take a lot to close down the interstate. But if they do, we'll just stay at your parents' place tonight."

"Won't that be wonderful."

"You can't be the first woman to bring home a former husband and a current fiancé for the night," Colby chided as he turned to give her a wink.

"Very funny."

"You have to admit, Colby's got a point," Grayson said.

"Whose fault is that?" she rejoined. "I've been against this from the beginning, but you two are the ones who've insisted."

"Grayson and I enjoy the same sense of drama." Colby chortled.

She gave him a dirty look. "I ought to drop you both off at the station and let you take the train home."

"You can't," Colby said. "You need me for your fortune and Grayson for your happiness."

Liz shook her head, mouthing the word *bastard*,"

which only made him laugh. The world might have thought they were the best of friends. Little did the world know.

CABOT FARM WAS on twenty wooded acres midway between Weston and Georgetown. It was nearly dark and was snowing quite heavily by the time the Lexus came to a stop at the foot of the long drive leading up to the house.

Grayson peered up the slope through the windshield. "It's either put on the chains or leave her here," he said. "I vote for leaving her here."

"Are we referring to Lizzy or the car?" Colby asked.

Liz leaned forward and whacked him on the shoulder. "I know I seem superfluous," she said, "but you two can't divide the oil rights without me. Besides, Mother would notice if I didn't show up."

They all laughed and climbed out of the car. Grayson put on his billed woolly cap and topcoat, Liz her beret and heavy coat. Only Colby was bareheaded, though he pulled up the collar of his topcoat. The driveway, which was little more than a track, was slippery, so they held hands going up the steep part, Liz between the two men. The falling snow was moist enough that it stuck to their hair and lashes.

Margaret Cabot was at the door of the large eighteenth-century farmhouse to greet them.

"I was afraid you wouldn't make it, but so glad that you did," she said cheerfully.

Liz embraced her. "Another two hours and we wouldn't have been able to get off the interstate."

Margaret allowed Grayson to kiss her cheek and, after briefly hesitating, offered her cheek to Colby, as well. Unlike the day before, when Margaret had put on her show at the Russian Tea Room, Liz was amused by her mother's forced affection with Colby.

"Leave your coats in the entry to dry," Margaret said, "and come have some hot mulled wine by the fire."

They went into the front room of the fine old house that exuded country elegance, with a mixture of quality antiques, lovely oil paintings and comfortable sofas and chairs. Weldon Cabot, a tall, heavyset man fifteen years his wife's senior, came from the den to join them. He wore a bulky cardigan and was smoking a pipe. He greeted Colby politely, but less effusively than his wife.

"Good to see you, Sommers. Good to see you," he said through puffs of smoke. "It's been a long time."

"Ten years," Colby said.

"That long?"

They gathered around the fire, Liz and Grayson sitting on the sofa, Colby and Weldon taking the wing chairs on either side of the fireplace. They talked about the storm as Margaret served the hot mulled wine to everyone except Weldon, who declined in favor of his usual Scotch.

Liz found the situation incredibly bizarre. She was in her parents' home, her fiancé was seated beside her and her ex was in the room, watching her every move with shining eyes and a faintly pained smile. The sofas and chairs had changed in the interim, but ten years earlier all of them but Grayson had sat in this very room, with the same grandfather clock ticking in the corner, as they negotiated the end to her ill-fated marriage.

When everyone had a drink, Margaret slipped onto the sofa next to Liz. She toasted their arrival, welcomed them all to her home and settled into silence. For a while the only sound in the room was the crackling of the fire. Weldon spoke, lamenting that the firewood wasn't as seasoned as it should be. Then he made a comment about the poor quality of modern goods in general before falling back to puffing on his pipe.

Liz watched Colby. She knew he had to be recalling his last visit, and the pain it must have caused him.

Margaret didn't allow the awkwardness to persist for long, launching into a recap of lunch at the Russian Tea Room and how delighted she'd been—and still was—by Colby's good news. Then Colby noted none of it would have happened had it not been for Virgil's shrewdness and foresight.

Mention of Virgil reminded Margaret of her own days in Texas. She spoke about them with more charity than she ever had previously. And when the conversation lapsed, Weldon pointedly blew a puff of smoke toward the ceilings and said to his wife, "Your mistake, my dear, was in not striking oil."

"I was too busy watching where I stepped," Margaret said with a laugh. She turned to Colby. "Liz tells me you have a ranch of your own, dear. Do you raise cattle?"

"Yes, ma'am."

"A large place, is it?" Weldon asked.

"Not by Texas standards," he replied. "I own four

thousand acres and have grazing rights to an additional six thousand."

"Sounds like a substantial holding to me. In Connecticut, it would just about make you a majority owner of the state."

They all laughed.

That got the conversation going in earnest. It came back around to the Continental American offer. Grayson shared the particulars with Weldon. The older man asked Colby how he proposed to exploit the opportunity.

"I've left the ball in Liz's court," he said, "but it seems to me the easiest and most efficient approach would be for us to remain partners."

Grayson noted there wouldn't be any management responsibility since the partnership would essentially be an investment vehicle. There'd be little or no need for decision-making, and therefore a formal partnership agreement. If they chose, they could simply remain co-owners, each with an undivided interest in the property.

"That's probably an advantage," Liz said, "especially for tax reasons."

"What would Continental American need from us under that scenario?" Colby asked.

"Both your signatures on the lease agreement," Grayson replied. "That's it."

"Sounds easy enough."

"We could instruct them to pay our half interests to each of us directly," Liz said.

"What about Virgil's house and the remaining land? Do you want to keep it or sell it?"

Colby was, in effect, asking if she had any interest in

maintaining a connection with Texas—and, by extension, with him. It was a question Liz had anticipated. "I think you should have it, Colby," she said.

He studied her. "You sayin' that out of generosity or self-interest?"

"Maybe a little of both," she replied, seeing that he'd understood her intent perfectly.

"Maybe Margaret would like it for sentimental reasons," he said, chuckling. "You once made your home there, didn't you, ma'am?"

"Good Lord, I still have nightmares about those side-turners or whatever you call them."

"Sidewinders," Colby said.

"Rattlesnakes, you mean," Weldon said with a puff of smoke.

"Yes, dear. Rattlesnakes. The day I stepped onto the porch and saw one hissing at me was the day I knew I badly needed a New England winter. I can't tell you how I hated the snakes."

"Dad must have cleared them out because I don't think I saw one the whole time I was in Texas," Liz said.

"In winter they're pretty scarce, Liz," Colby explained.

"Oh."

"In summer you just avoid sleeping on the floor," he said with a laugh.

Margaret shivered and said they needed a change of topic. Weldon got up to add wood to the fire. Grayson asked Margaret which of her delightful dishes she'd planned for dinner, and Liz and Colby looked at each other.

He seemed a bit wistful to her. She sensed he was

thinking about a particular winter on Virgil Gibson's ranch—the one ten years earlier when she'd made one of her treks between the main house and the bunkhouse.

When Grayson and Margaret went off in search of more hot mulled wine and Weldon ambled into his den to fetch more pipe tobacco, Liz and Colby found themselves alone.

"You're even prettier than the last time I saw you by firelight," he said.

"Oh?" The compliment caught her by surprise. "When was that?"

"Here in this room. The night before they sent me packing."

"There was a fire that night?"

"Yes."

"I remember the ticking clock," she said, glancing over at the sonorous grandfather clock that had been in her mother's family for generations.

"Me, too."

"Does being here make you feel bitter?"

Colby shook his head. "More sad than bitter. It's not something you want to hear, I know, but I still think what happened was unnecessary."

"But yesterday you told Mother she'd been right about us."

"That was for her benefit."

Weldon returned, puffing on his pipe. "So, Sommers," he said, "the last ten years have brought you good fortune."

"I'm doing okay, sir."

"Raise cattle mostly?"

"That and fiddle with investments. Virgil did well

by it. I decided to borrow a leaf from his book, so to speak."

Weldon was about to drop back into his chair when the phone rang. He looked back toward the kitchen, then decided the phone might not be answered. "I'd better get that. Excuse me."

He tottered off, leaving Liz and Colby alone again.

"It must give you some satisfaction having everybody catering to you now that you're rich."

"They're doing it for the wrong reasons, Liz, so I don't put much stock in it."

"I suppose you feel that way about me, as well."

Colby arched a brow. "I believe your renewed interest in me predated the discovery of oil."

She looked away.

"And that's a source of great satisfaction to me," he went on. "The high point of the trip, as far as I'm concerned."

"Well, much as I don't like talking about it, I admit it would have been terrible if you thought I'd done that because of your money," she said. "If nothing else, at least my timing was good."

"Actually, I'm still trying to figure out what happened."

Liz looked at him, wanting to tell him he knew perfectly well what it was—a fling, an adventure. Just sex. But that wasn't something they could discuss now. She didn't have the energy or the will to demean it, anyway.

Grayson and Margaret returned with more hot mulled wine. At the same moment Weldon shuffled to the door, a rather serious expression on his face.

"Grayson," he said, "there's a call from your brother. It is urgent, I'm afraid."

There was a moment of stunned silence. Grayson put the mugs he was carrying down on the coffee table and went off to the den without a word.

"What could that be?" Margaret said when he was gone.

Liz explained that his mother was in the hospital in Boston. Margaret and Weldon were duly sobered. After a couple of minutes with nothing being said, the only sound coming from the fire and the clock ticking, Grayson returned, his face ashen.

"I'm afraid Mother's had a setback," he announced. "They think another stroke."

"Oh, no," Margaret and Liz said almost in unison.

"It's not life threatening at the moment, but Darren thinks I should be there. Considering the storm, the train seems the best bet. When's the next one? Do you know, Weldon?"

Cabot looked at the clock. "We should call to confirm, but I think you could get a train in Bridgeport in a little less than an hour."

"I'd have to leave right away."

Liz got up, taking his arm. "Do you want me to go with you?"

"No, there's no point. You don't have anything with you. I can easily stay with Darren. The important thing is that I be there for Mother. She's looked to me since Father died. Even more than to Darren."

"Let me confirm the train," Margaret said, going off.

"Considering the storm, we'd better take you to the station in my Land Rover," Weldon said. "It's your best chance of getting through. Unfortunately, I'm not much of a driver at night, even in good conditions. Perhaps someone else could..."

"Colby and I can drive him," Liz said. "Don't worry about that." She put her arm around Grayson. "I'm so sorry about your mother."

"I feel terrible about leaving. Margaret has such a lovely dinner planned."

"First things first."

Margaret returned to the sitting room. "You have fifty minutes before the next train," she announced.

"Let me get the keys to my vehicle," Weldon said.

"Grayson," Margaret said, "you're going to have a bowl of soup while they get the car out of the garage." She took his arm. "Come with me."

They went off to the kitchen.

Liz and Colby found themselves alone again. Liz worried for Grayson's mother, but a part of her was pleased by the prospect of being alone with Colby.

"Fate is a curious thing," he said.

"Yes, isn't it?"

"I suppose it would be insensitive of me to say I wish we didn't have to come back for dinner."

"Yes," she said nodding, "it would be insensitive."

COLBY WAS used to handling four-wheel vehicles in difficult terrain, sometimes even with snow on the ground, but not snow like this. Weldon Cabot's Land Rover handled the conditions well. The hardest part was figuring out where the road was. Liz sat in front to help navigate. Grayson, who clearly was concerned about his mother, sat in back. He was mostly silent.

Once they got to Bridgeport, driving was easier. They arrived at the station with twelve minutes to spare. Liz got out and went with Grayson to the entrance. Colby sat watching them, his attention focused on Liz's body language.

He was convinced now that she and Grayson did not belong together and knew her decision to marry him had been made with her head, not her heart. Colby decided if her willingness to go to bed with him wasn't proof enough, what he'd observed of the couple told him everything he needed to know.

But he also knew that Liz was stubborn. She'd married him out of stubbornness, then left him for the same reason. It was obvious she was on the same sort of path now. The difference was she was being pulled by her logic, not her feelings.

Liz returned to the Land Rover, bringing a rush of cold into the cab with her. She took a fatigued breath as she stared straight ahead. Colby knew the exhaustion she was feeling was largely emotional.

"You okay?" he asked.

Liz gave him a tired, grateful smile. "I'll survive."

Colby started the car and began retracing their route back to the Cabot farm. Liz said little, except to give directions.

"We're going to have to stay with my parents tonight," she said. "There's no way we can make it back to New York."

"That's okay. It wouldn't be the first time I've spent the night at your parents'."

"I'm curious, Colby. Are you being a good sport, or is it a matter of having the last laugh?"

"A little of both."

"You could rub it in a lot more than you have. I admire your restraint."

They fell silent. Liz's proximity was torture, especially now that they were alone, yet there was nothing he could do to act on his feelings.

"The only thing I feel badly about is you marrying Grayson," he said, figuring he might as well get his thoughts on the table.

Liz looked at him.

"It's not exactly jealousy," he went on. "It's more that I think you're making a bad mistake."

"I'm going to marry him."

"I know you're determined, Liz, but it's for all the wrong reasons."

"How would you know my reasons?"

"You're forcing it. It's obvious. Your brain is pulling you along like a kid dragging a reluctant puppy out to play."

"Maybe that's wishful thinking on your part. Maybe you made the mistake of thinking that Thursday night meant something."

"Oh, it meant something. We both know that it did. We just aren't agreed on what."

"I was very upset afterward," she said. "I felt terrible. But now that I've gotten it into perspective I feel better."

"You've rationalized, that's all."

"You seem awfully sure of yourself," she said.

"I am."

"Tell me, then. What do *you* think it meant? We're always talking about me and my feelings. How about you? You don't really think it had meaning beyond the obvious, do you?"

"I think you have needs you aren't willing to admit to, Liz."

"I have a weakness, yes. Maybe a moral blind spot, as well."

"You can't pass it off as the act of a loose woman," he said. "How many other guys have you slept with since you've known Grayson?"

She said nothing.

"You aren't answering the question."

"None!" she snapped.

"None. Well, maybe there's a lesson in that."

"Sure there is, Colby. You're irresistible. I have this inability to avoid throwing myself at you. You're the lover I can't say no to. If you were around all the time, I'd want to get in bed with you every chance I got. There. Are you happy now?"

"I'm just a piece of meat to you and don't mean a thing. Is that what you're trying to say?"

"I love Grayson."

"I don't buy it."

"Let me rephrase it. Grayson is the sort of man I need. We're of the same world. We do the same things, value the same things. You're a fantasy, Colby. You're causing me fits now, but in time I know you'll pass. I'm playing this for the long run. Did you hear me? The *long run*. It's as simple as that."

"Somehow I get the feeling there's a message in this for me."

"Only what I've said."

"No, there's more," he said. "You want me to make it easy for you to marry Grayson."

"I want you to understand."

"To spare my feelings?"

Liz sighed with exasperation. "Since you seem to

know everything, why don't you tell me what you think?"

"No, Liz," he said, "I'm telling you what I'm going to do. Monday morning I'm going into Continental American and signing the papers. Then I'm getting on the next plane for San Antonio. If you sign the papers, the deal will be done. All I have to do then is wait for my check in the mail. It's what Grayson would like, I know. And he's right. It's simple. It's clean."

"And we won't have to deal with each other," she said. "That's what you're really saying, isn't it?"

"It's what you want, Liz. You want to do your thing in New York while I do mine at home in Texas."

"You're making it all sound so heartless."

"Sweetheart," he said with a smile. "I'm stating the cold hard facts."

Liz had to admit he was making it easy for her. What more could she ask for? So why was she unhappy?

"I wish things were different," she said. "That we were different people."

"We are who we are, Lizzy. Accept the fact."

She didn't like it, but he was right. Ironically, that made it worse. Why couldn't Colby make her hate him? That would be better.

The blizzard became so intense that they had to stop. Colby could scarcely see past the hood of the Land Rover.

"Lordy," he said, "I've never seen so much snow in my life."

"It may let up."

After a few minutes the fury abated a little and they were able to see the shadowy profiles of the trees lining the road. Colby put the vehicle in gear and they started creeping along. Liz looked out her side to help guide him as best she could.

"At this rate we won't make it home till morning," she said.

"If worse comes to worst, you can drive and I'll get out and lead the way on foot. We can't have much more than two or three miles to go."

Liz checked out what she could see of the terrain, looking for a landmark. "That's about right."

The wind rose again and the swirling snow again reached the point of a whiteout. It became impossible to go on. Colby set the hand brake.

"So close and yet so far," he said. "Do you want to try following my lead on foot?"

"You're not dressed for it. It'd take hours and you'd freeze to death."

"The one time I decide to play city slicker and don't have my boots on. Wouldn't you know?"

She didn't want to say so, but she was glad. She'd liked seeing him looking like a regular guy, even if it was a sort of costume in reverse. "I thought you looked very nice today," she told him.

"That's not the practical Liz Cabot I know and love."

She knew he was chiding her, but she could hardly complain. Colby gazed at her in the near darkness, seeing the earnest expression on her face.

"Doesn't part of you wish things were different?" she said.

"In what way?"

"Maybe what I mean to say is, I wish we weren't so ill suited for each other."

"Sweetheart, we are who we are. But don't worry,"

he said, patting her knee, "in a couple of days I'll be gone."

She bowed her head.

"But first we have to decide what to do now. Do you want to slog it out or sit it out? I'm game either way."

"There's a bed-and-breakfast place about quarter of a mile back down the road. I saw the sign. At the very least, we can call my parents from there and let them know what's happened."

"If I can turn this baby around, it'll be a miracle, but nothing ventured, nothing gained," Colby said. "The worst that can happen, I guess, is we sit out the night in the ditch."

It took some effort, and Liz getting out to guide him, but they managed to do a U-turn. It was mostly down-hill going back and they had the advantage of being able to see their tracks in the snow.

Despite the fact they were barely moving, they al-most passed the driveway. Liz spotted the sign at the last moment. Colby had to back up a bit, but he made the turn. It was a hundred feet to the house, but they couldn't see lights until they were within fifty feet.

The elderly woman who greeted them at the door and admitted them into the entry was shocked to see them. "Heavens, I can't believe a soul would be out in this weather."

"The question is if there's room at the inn," Colby said, stomping his feet on the chunk of rag carpet, meant for snowy shoes and boots, situated by the door.

"I haven't a single guest, so you're in luck," the woman said. She was small, bundled in sweaters and a long wool skirt and heavy stockings. "Take off your coats and come warm yourselves by the fire."

When they'd settled in the cozy parlor, the woman who introduced herself as Mrs. Williamson explained the accommodations she had available. "I have three rooms upstairs in the main house that share a bath. There's a cottage in back with private bath, sitting room and fireplace. Weekends, it goes for a hundred-twenty per night. Double rooms are sixty. Considering the storm, you can have any of the rooms for half-price."

"Fair enough," Colby said. "We'll take the cottage."

Liz, who was sitting near the fire, gave him a side-ward glance but said nothing.

"It's a lovely cottage," Mrs. Williamson said. "The last people to occupy it was a young couple from Bridgeport who were married on Valentine's Day and spent their wedding night here. There are a dozen long-stem roses the couple brought with them still in the cottage. As the young lady said, they could hardly take them to Jamaica. But now you can enjoy them."

"Sounds perfect, ma'am," Colby said, giving Liz a wink.

"Would it be possible for me to use your phone?" Liz asked the woman. "It's a local call."

"Certainly, dear. I'll show you the phone and get the key to the cottage. You'll have to trudge through a bit of snow, I'm afraid."

"No problem," Liz said. "Colby can carry me. He's such a gentleman."

TO HER AMAZEMENT, Colby did carry her through the snow. If she'd had any doubts before as to where things were leading, she didn't now. Colby seemed to have finally accepted the inevitability of their separate destinies. This was to be their final night, their last fare-well.

The cottage was nestled under what in the summer must have been the boughs of huge shade trees. In the blowing snow, she could barely make out the icy branches overhead.

Brushing the snow off the tiny porch with his shoe, Colby set her down and opened the door with the key Mrs. Williamson had given him. Liz was shivering by the time they got inside.

The landlady had warned them that the heat would just be high enough to keep the inside temperature above freezing, so they'd have to turn up the wall heater to maximum and build a fire. While Liz turned on a lamp and fiddled with the heater, Colby started the fire. Once he'd gotten the flames going, he took off his coat and wet shoes. Liz knelt next to him as he nursed the fire.

"Do you think I'm depraved?" she said.

"Depraved? Why do you ask?"

"Because I could have insisted on separate rooms."

"But you didn't, did you?"

"Why do you think I didn't, Colby?"

He gave her an impatient look. "Sweetheart, do you really think it's a good idea to analyze this to death? It's what you want, isn't it?"

Liz sat back on her heels. "Yes, but I don't like you making it sound like some kind of..."

"Some kind of what?"

"I don't know...business deal or something."

"Look, don't go making something out of this that it isn't," he said. "You've already said where your long-term plan will take you. This is the short-term plan. It's that simple."

"You're taking the romance right out of it," she complained. "Don't you see I need to know that you want me as badly as I want you."

"That's never been our problem, sugar."

Liz stared at him, unsure whether he was punishing her or just trying to protect his own ego. She suddenly realized this wasn't right. She was forcing it. "Colby," she said, "maybe this is a mistake."

"So far, nothing's happened," he replied, taking off his wet socks. "We've taken shelter from the storm. No sin in that."

"I thought I wanted to make love with you, but now I'm not so sure."

She watched him spread his socks out on the hearth to dry. He began rubbing his toes as he held them to the fire, warming them. "I'm a gentleman. As matter of fact I was a gentleman when we were married."

She nodded. "I know you were."

"So you're safe."

She shook her head. "I've just had a terrible realization. This is all my fault. It was my fault ten years ago and it's my fault now. I *am* depraved. To anybody else it'd be obvious. But I'm just now figuring it out."

He took her chin in his hand. "Don't go soft on me, Lizzy. There's not a damned thing wrong with you."

"You're patronizing me."

"I'm trying to be considerate."

"Whether you know it or not, you're letting me know how much you disapprove of me. You don't respect me. You feel contempt."

He stared at the fire, watching the flames. Liz

watched the shadows playing on his face. His expression was sad. "You're wrong," he said after several moments. "I loved you, Liz. The darkest day of my life was when I got in my truck and went home to Texas without you. I suppose, if I were a hundred percent honest, I'd have to say I feel pretty much the same way about you now. The only difference is my skin's a little thicker since I've grown up, and I understand you better."

A lump formed in her throat the size of a grapefruit. It was all she could do to keep from throwing herself in his arms. She didn't want him saying he loved her. She wanted him saying he couldn't resist her, that he had to make love to her because he couldn't help himself.

Colby added wood to the fire, then turned his socks over. The fire was getting warm. Liz moved back to one of the matching chintz armchairs that were drawn up to the hearth. Colby stood to dry his pants. She stared up at him, feeling the most pain she'd had since that night nearly ten years ago when she'd told him she no longer wanted to be his wife.

"I thought I was a happy, well-adjusted woman with my life on track," she said, "until..."

"Until what?"

"Until Thursday night when you got out of that taxicab and walked back into my life."

"I was feeling pretty good about myself, too."

"You see how bad we are for each other?" she said, her voice shaking. She was about to break into tears.

"Yeah, no doubt about it. We're both poison."

Colby sat in the other chair. For a minute or two he stared at the fire. Liz did, as well, her heart aching. Then he reached out and took her hand.

"Think of it this way," he said, "as soon as I get on that plane, you'll be free."

Tears began rolling down her cheeks. She did nothing to wipe them away. He looked toward the window as the wind shook the glass. She shivered, rubbing her arms.

"I want to go to bed," she whispered. "Will you come with me?"

"I think I'll just sit here for a while, Lizzy. There's still some cold in my bones."

Liz slipped out of the chair and went to the bedroom. She undressed, then slid under the covers. The sheets felt icy and she shivered violently. But after a while she began to warm up. She lay, listening to the crackle of the fire in the next room, watching the shadows from the firelight dancing on the ceiling.

Waiting for him, she began an imaginary conversation. "Do you remember when we'd walk by those big homes in the Garden District in New Orleans, dreaming what it would be like to live in one and have somebody bring us lemonade on a silver tray? Remember how we used to pretend?"

Then in her mind she heard him say, "We could afford one of those places now, Lizzy. In fact, we could afford a whole block of them, if we wanted to."

"And here we are, in bed, confused about what we want, what this means..." And then she imagined him touching her, arousing her. She imagined them kissing, losing themselves in the moment.

But then the crackling fire intruded. Liz lifted her head to see what he was doing. Colby hadn't moved. Nor did it appear he intended to, anytime soon. Only then did it occur to her that he wasn't coming to bed. He'd decided to end things a different way. They would never make love again.

11

June

"MY GOD," Wendy Goldstein said as they got up from the table, "do you girls realize every one of us is in a sleeveless dress and carrying a white purse tonight?"

"Liz's is more beige," Angela said.

"Picky, picky. The point is we're starting to look like a Girl Scout troop."

"And we're sounding like one sometimes, too," Ariel intoned. "Since Moira is leaving us, I say we replace her with a man. A confirmed bachelor. It'll spice things up a little."

"Leave it to you to come up with a suggestion like that," Angela said.

"There's no shortage of confirmed bachelors," Pam said to Ariel. "The trick is finding *un*confirmed ones."

"You're doing all right, Miss Hotpants," Ariel replied. "I don't know what you're complaining about."

Everybody glanced at Liz. It was common knowledge that Pam Wilson had begun dating Grayson Bartholomew, a situation that was unprecedented in the Thursday Night Club. More than one woman in the group had dated the same guy before, but for someone to be dating the former fiancé of another member was a first.

Liz, of course, wasn't bothered by the situation.

She'd been the one to break her engagement with Grayson in March, but it did make for a bit of awkwardness. When Pam had skipped a meeting following an embarrassing moment she and Liz had experienced involving Grayson, Liz decided she needed to clear the air. She'd asked Pam out to lunch and assured her that there was no reason Grayson should be a problem between them. "Grayson deserves a relationship with someone just as nice as he is," Liz told her. "I really don't want the fact that he and I were engaged to get in the way of my friendship with you."

Pam had appreciated Liz's understanding. Liz had felt better, too. She'd meant every word of what she'd said, but she couldn't help feeling a twinge whenever she saw Pam and Grayson together. After all, she had cared for him, and she still considered him a fine man. But if running into Colby Sommers back in February had proven anything, it was that she couldn't marry Grayson.

She'd told Moira that if she were ever to marry, it would be to a guy who engendered passion in her the way Colby did, yet fit into her world like Grayson. "A tall order," Moira had replied.

Liz looked over at her best friend. Everybody was giving her a hug and saying their farewells. Moira was crying. It was not only her last meeting of the Thursday Night Club for Divorcées, Spinsters and Other Reprobates, but Moira was leaving New York for her hometown in Ohio where the wedding was to be held. Then, after a honeymoon, she and Larry would be moving to Kansas City where he was to take over as the new Assistant Superintendent of Schools.

Moira had talked to Liz about possibly being in the

wedding party, but because the wedding was to be small, she decided in the end only to have one bridesmaid, her younger sister. "The important thing is that I'm there for your big day," Liz had assured her.

The women began filing out. Liz hung back, waiting for Moira to turn to her. They smiled at each other as Moira dabbed her eyes. Then they embraced.

"I never thought this day would come," Moira said.

"At this rate, you aren't going to have any tears left for the wedding, kiddo."

They held each other. "Four months ago, who'd have thought *you* would be seeing *me* off at *my* last meeting?"

"Life has a way of pulling surprises."

Moira brushed back her red hair and put her handkerchief in her purse. They headed for the door. Moira took Liz's arm as they walked toward the stairs.

"Do you hate me being the last of the Mohicans as much as I hated you?" Moira asked.

"I think it's a little different because I'm here by choice. I could be getting married in a few weeks myself, don't forget."

"But you're going to have to hear about Grayson from Pam for the next umpteen weeks. That can't make it any easier."

"Pam and I have an understanding. Anyway, before long, one of two things will happen. They'll either split up, or marry. Either way, the problem will be solved."

They came to the stairs and started up.

"I'm constantly amazed at how stoic you've been," Moira said. "I know you have to be suffering more than you admit."

"I kind of asked for it. Anyway, Grayson deserves

someone who loves him passionately. Pam might be the one."

"What about Colby?"

"What about him?"

"You never talk about him."

"I learned last time we were together that there's nothing to be gained by dwelling on my feelings toward him. Colby will always live in my memory, and I've got to learn to accept that and go on."

"That's too philosophical for my taste."

"Everybody deals with things in their own way."

They arrived at the lobby. Looking out the main doors, they could see Wendy and Angela climbing into a cab. They made their way to the entrance. Outside, it was a lovely early-summer evening.

"Want to walk for a while?" Moira asked.

"I thought you were meeting Larry."

"I have some time. Half an hour, anyway."

"I'd better savor every minute I've got with you," Liz said. "There won't be any more Thursday nights. Not with my best friend, anyway."

"Stop it, or I'm going to start crying again."

They started up the street, heading north. Liz looked up at the pinkish hue in the high clouds overhead. She liked New York this time of year, before the dog days of summer set in. "Will the weather be like this in Ohio?" she asked.

"More or less."

"I've never been to Cleveland, but I have to tell you, it seems like a damned inconvenient place to have a wedding."

"When you live in New York, the rest of the world seems inconvenient.

"Tell me about it," Liz said.

She could feel Moira's eyes on her and was afraid to look because she didn't want to see her pity. Moira had worried about her the past several months. Tonight she seemed especially concerned, perhaps because she was leaving. Liz, for her part, felt a bit more unsettled than she wanted to admit.

Ever since her fling with Colby Sommers, things had not quite been the same. Liz had been living with the feeling she had this big hole in her. At first she'd attributed it to the breakup with Grayson. Then she'd realized it had more to do with Colby.

"Why don't you write him?" Moira said as they tripped along.

"Who? Colby?"

"Yes, of course."

"Oh, Moira, you're a worse romantic than he is."

Moira gave her a double-take. "Has Colby written to you?"

"No."

"Then what did you mean?"

"I don't know what I meant. It's just that thinking about him is pointless. I guess that's what I was trying to say."

"Colby told you he loved you, didn't he?"

"Damn it, Moira," Liz said, giving her a look. "You're a troublemaker."

"I knew it was something. Colby told you he still loved you and you can't get that out of your mind."

"It doesn't change a thing."

"I think you're afraid," Moira said.

"Afraid of what?"

"Your feelings."

"I can't see that anything has changed from ten years ago."

"And so you're going to wait and see if you happen to run into him again somewhere. Maybe on your twentieth anniversary?"

"Moira," she said, surprised, "are you being sarcastic?"

"I'm sorry, I guess I don't like seeing you do this to yourself."

"Do what? I'm fine. I don't need someone in my life to be happy. My career's going well. Even my mother says I shouldn't have married Grayson if I didn't love him the right way."

They stopped at the corner to wait for the light to change.

"That's good then," Moira said. "If you're happy, I'm happy."

"You just feel guilty because you're abandoning me," Liz chided.

"Yeah, we all hate to give up our lives for a man, but we do it, don't we?"

The light changed and they started across the street, dodging a taxi hurtling around the corner. Moira shook her head.

"Some things about New York I won't miss."

They went along the street, stopping for a moment to look in the window of a shoe store. Moira peered in the shop.

"I'm having a hell of a time finding the right shoes."

"I'm sure you'll find what you need in Cleveland," Liz said, poking her in the ribs.

"Bitchy, bitchy," Moira said.

· They continued up the walk. Liz again looked up at
the sky.

"Maybe I should make a confession," she said. "I
haven't completely ignored Colby's existence."

"That's hardly a surprise."

"No, what I mean is I sort of made a halfhearted
overture to him."

Moira's brows rose in surprise. "What kind of overture?"

"You know that recreation hall I donated to that
boys' home in my father's name?"

"The one in Texas? The one the state senator wrote
you a letter about?"

"Yes."

"What about it?"

"Well, in a few weeks they're having a ground-
breaking ceremony and they invited me to come. It's a
couple of days after your wedding. I'm going to fly
from Cleveland to San Antonio for the ceremony."

"And?"

"And I suggested they invite Colby. I have no idea if
they will, and even if they do, I don't know that he'd
come, but I made an effort."

Moira had a knowing smile.

"I'm not sure why I did it," Liz said. "I guess it was
in a moment of weakness."

"Friday nights alone can do that to you. Believe me,
I remember.

"So, what are you going to do if he shows up?"
Moira asked.

"I don't know. See what happens, I guess."

"What would you like to have happen?"

"Moira, quit being so logical. I haven't gotten that far

yet. It took a lot of courage to do what I've done. For all I know, Colby's met somebody and he's in love. He left New York without any hope that we might have a future, I can tell you that."

Moira had already heard the story. Liz didn't have to repeat it. The drive with Colby back to the city after the snowstorm had been one of the most painful experiences of her life. Although he'd tried to cover it up with politeness, she knew she'd hurt him—that was obvious.

When Colby had said goodbye to her, sitting in Grayson's car outside the Clairbourne, she could see in his eyes that she had disappointed him greatly.

"If I've learned anything in life, Colby, it's that you can't go back."

"Well, if I've learned anything in life," he replied, "it's that people can have a change of heart. We all grow, after all. Some of us a lot more than others."

Liz had already made her decision to break up with Grayson during that sleepless night in the cottage. But she hadn't told Colby then—it had seemed only right that she talk to Grayson first, and she couldn't do that until the emergency with his mother had passed. Besides, she'd seen no reason not to leave Colby with the impression she would still marry.

Being a gentleman, he'd wished her well. At the end, she could see that he'd finally written her off. She couldn't blame him.

But as the weeks rolled past she'd thought about his remark that people could have a change of heart. She'd rejected the notion that there could ever be anything between them, because they came from such disparate places and had such different lives. Then she'd thought about how good she'd felt when she was with Colby and how uncomfortable around Grayson, in comparison.

At the same time she knew that people who were the life of the party weren't always the best company at breakfast. As her mother liked to say, "The way a man likes his eggs is a lot more critical than the way he kisses." At eighteen Liz hadn't understood that, but after several years of life, she'd come to understand what her mother meant was that daily life determined the outcome of a marriage more than the high points. And Colby was memorable for the high points.

"Well, to me," Moira said, "what people do is a lot more important than what people say. My dad calls it 'walking your talk.' Personally I think it's telling that you got Colby invited to that dedication ceremony."

"Weakness of the flesh, Moira. That's what it means."

The redhead shrugged. "Have it your way. But if I were in your shoes, I'd ask myself why you're fighting it so hard."

"That sounds like something Colby would say."

"In that case Colby must be a heck of a smart guy."

They had a good laugh about that.

Moira had to go then if she were to meet Larry on time. Seeing a taxi, she flagged it down. Then she and Liz embraced.

"Next stop Cleveland," Liz said, tears filling her eyes.

Moira was teary again, too. "It means so much to me that you're coming to the wedding."

"I wouldn't miss it for the world."

"I love you, Liz."

"I love you, too, Moira. Give my best to Larry."

Moira folded her long legs into the taxi. She waved. "I will."

The taxi took off up the street and Liz was alone. She stepped back as a bus went by, spewing fumes. Then she started walking again, glancing up at the darkening sky. Out in Texas, Colby might at that very moment be looking at the sky. Perhaps he was on horseback or sitting on his porch listening to the cicadas.

It was probably wishful thinking, but she wondered if maybe Colby was remembering her. Dreaming, she realized, could be a very dangerous business. No telling where it could take you—maybe even to Texas and a change of heart.

12

July

LIZ HAD GOTTEN a map of Texas and refreshed her memory of where places were relative to one another. Fredericksburg, the nearest town to the boys' home, was closer to San Antonio than she recalled, but Fort McKavett, the postal address for Colby's ranch, was still a good deal farther west. After studying the map, she realized it would take a special effort on his part to attend.

The rental-car agent at the airport in San Antonio told her the best bet for a motel was along the interstate, but Liz decided to go into Fredericksburg. The town was about twenty miles off I-10. She ended up in a modest little motel on the edge of town, arriving just before dusk.

It was a nice evening, so Liz decided to walk in the balmy air to the local coffee shop. The restaurant was a carbon copy of many she'd seen, with worn stainless-steel appliances, cracked vinyl booths and homemade pies in a mirrored glass case. Liz had a chicken fried steak, mashed potatoes and peas.

Looking around at the other diners, she saw men in baseball caps or cowboy hats and jeans. The women wore jeans or flowered cotton dresses, depending on their age.

Liz noticed a young woman with a tanned face and ponytail and a T-shirt that read The Answer's No— What's the Question? sitting at the counter with a gangly cowboy. It depressed her to think that that could have been Liz herself, had she come back to Texas with Colby ten years ago. Not that the woman seemed unhappy, but her life did seem limited.

Not that Liz was arrogant enough to think herself superior. She knew there were good people and bad people everywhere. Nor was it a matter of wealth. As her dad once told her when they'd stopped in town, "Half the codgers around here are millionaires, Lizzy, but you'd never know it to look at 'em. They wear manure on their boots and drink their coffee from a fifty-cent mug, same as everybody else."

If there was an issue, it was life-style—how she'd spend her days. Which was the real Liz Cabot—an evening concert of chamber music or a country barbecue?

This was her first trip to Texas since the breakup of her marriage and it brought back powerful memories, some good, some bad. At a visceral level, the simplicity and honesty of down-home living felt good—maybe it was the Gibson blood in her veins. And yet, she had to ask herself, was this enough? The answer, of course, was no.

Walking through the quiet streets of Fredericksburg, back to her motel, Liz wondered if it hadn't been a mistake to have Colby invited to the ground-breaking ceremony. He'd look good to her—she already knew that. But what could she say to him? What had changed? Not her feelings. She'd always loved him in her way, but all they had was a past, not a future.

At the wedding reception the day before, Moira had

taken Liz aside and said, "Have a good time in Texas. Let down your hair."

At one level, Liz had to agree it sounded like good advice. But wasn't that what she'd done ten years ago? Look what had happened. And hadn't her mother made the same mistake?

Still, here she was, less than a hundred miles from Colby Sommers, eager to see him, wondering what, if anything, would happen when she did. Liz knew that deep down inside she was afraid. Which would rule her, she wondered—her head or her heart?

She had carefully watched the guests at Moira's wedding. They were midwesterners, not Texans, but she'd seen the same sort of wholesome simplicity in them. Moira had been able to go home, marry and start a new life. How had she done it? Was it because her heart had never really left Ohio? Were those eight years she'd spent in the bright lights of New York just a long vacation? Would she be happy in Kansas City?

Back at the motel, Liz took a bath. Amazingly, she found herself humming the western tune she'd heard at the diner. She'd never cared much for country-and-western music. Oddly enough she couldn't say if Colby favored it or not.

The water had to be from a well because it had a strong mineral scent. Liz wiggled her toes and listened to the cooing of turtledoves in a tree outside the bathroom window, wondering about the odd twists of fate that had brought her here. The next day might well turn out to be a big nothing. Or it could be one of the most pivotal of her life.

COLBY DIDN'T SHOW UP at the ceremony. Liz sat on the little platform with the local dignitaries, listening to their speeches and the undeserved praise that was heaped upon her. But the whole time her eyes searched the crowd of a hundred adults and eighty boys sitting impatiently on folding chairs in the hot sun.

She gave a brief speech about her father, her eyes getting misty and her voice trembling when she spoke of discovering after his death what a good and decent man he'd been. "Virgil Gibson had no pretensions," she told the crowd, "but he was wise and shrewd and strong in his own quiet way. He had the spirit of a man in touch with the land, the kind of spirit every boy needs to find peace in his life." Then she told them she hoped that the Virgil Gibson Recreation Hall would help each of the boys at the home find the spirit inside them.

Her remarks had been brief, and oddly enough, many of the thoughts that had come to her about her father could have been said about Colby. That shouldn't have been a surprise. They'd been close and Colby had once told her he'd learned some of his most important lessons from Virgil Gibson.

After the speeches, the home's director, Mr. Quick, and a state senator who'd been an orphan, each turned a spade of dirt on the spot where the building would be erected. Afterward, Mr. Quick took Liz and the senator over to the table they'd set up under a big shade tree. A dark-haired girl with a shy smile poured them some inexpensive champagne.

As Liz drank, she took another last look at the parking lot. There were no late arrivals. She decided to take the bull by the horns and ask Mr. Quick if he'd sent Colby Sommers an invitation, as she'd requested.

"Yes, ma'am," Quick said. "It was the only name you gave me, so it could hardly be overlooked."

"I don't suppose you heard from him?"

"No, ma'am. It wasn't the sort of invitation that needed to be accepted."

"I understand."

Liz chatted with some of the boys and members of the staff. She was given a tour of the facility and, seeing there was still no sign of Colby, she decided it was time to go. Mr. Quick had invited her to join him and his wife and the senator for dinner that evening, but Liz begged off, saying she had a seat on the evening flight to New York.

After checking out of her motel and leaving Fredericksburg, Liz drove south on Highway 87 to Comfort and the interstate. At the interchange she had two choices. Eighty miles to the west in the direction of El Paso was the town of Junction. Thirty miles north of there was Fort McKavett. East on the interstate was San Antonio, the airport and her flight home. She was at a fork in the road, both literally and figuratively.

At a stop sign, she flirted with the idea of going west, rationalizing that a sentimental visit to her father's place wouldn't hurt. No need to actually call on Colby. But in the midst of her vacillation a big hay truck pulled up behind her, tooting its horn. Liz stepped on the gas and proceeded to the eastbound on-ramp. The hay truck had decided for her.

When she got back, she'd drop Colby a note. He would probably appreciate hearing about the recreation hall. She could suggest he stop by and have a look sometime. But that was transparent, of course. Her only reason for writing would be to make contact, and if Colby had cared, he'd have gone to the ceremony. No, this was goodbye to Texas, unless she came back for the dedication of the building. If so, she wouldn't invite Colby. He'd spoken.

She was approaching an exit and suddenly swerved off the highway, sending up a cloud of dust. She sat there, unsure why she'd done what she'd done.

"Damn it," she shouted angrily, hitting the steering wheel. "Damn you, Colby Sommers! Why can't you leave me alone?"

DURING THE HOUR and fifteen minutes it took her to drive to the town of Junction, Liz decided she'd go to her father's ranch for a short visit. Then she'd call Colby and tell him she was in the neighborhood. If he invited her to come by, she would only if she sensed he truly meant it. If not, she'd be on the morning flight for New York.

Once she'd passed Junction, the terrain was more familiar. Liz recognized the exit at Ranch Road 2291. The town of Cleo, consisting of nothing more than a few scattered houses, was five miles off the interstate. To get to her father's place she had to turn at Cleo and drive west past Turkey Hollow, Walnut Canyon and Gilliam Draw. The names alone sent shivers of recollection through her bones. Memories.

The ranch road she was following dropped from higher ground covered with live oak, juniper and piñon pine to the open bottom land where Virgil Gibson's house was situated. Colby'd told her the place had been vacant for months. Finding a tenant wouldn't be easy, though the grazing land was easily enough leased.

Coming over a rise, Liz saw the house a quarter of a mile off the road. She followed the rutted track through a draw and up to the house. There was no sign of habitation.

A funny feeling went through her. The last time she'd seen this house it was from the passenger seat of her mother's rental car. Her dad was on the porch, looking dour as he waved goodbye, his favorite dog, Toby, at his feet. Now, Virgil and Toby were both gone, the windows of the house boarded up.

Liz got out and walked across the dry, dusty ground, circling the house in the hot afternoon sun. To her relief, the bunkhouse was still standing, though a corner of the roof looked partially caved in and the door was hanging from its hinges. She sat on the back stoop of the house and stared at the little shack that had been the place where she and Colby had consummated their love.

Liz got up and walked slowly toward the bunkhouse. Parched dust rose from her footsteps. The first time she'd walked over this ground it had been through a thin, powdery blanket of snow. The recollection was enough to make her shiver, despite the heat.

She stepped into what had once been Colby's home. The place held only a broken chair, a moldy mattress and a few empty cardboard boxes. Half the windowpanes were broken. It was a sad symbol of a bygone era in her life. And yet, the ghosts of the past had a strong presence. Liz had once lived a fairy tale on this spot.

She heard the hoofbeats for half a minute before she realized what they were, her mind adrift between the past and the present. The yapping dog finally jolted her into full awareness.

Liz went to the door and saw the rider and his mount stop in a billowing cloud of dust. A dog ran straight for the bunkhouse, barking. As the dust drifted off, she saw the man coming toward her, his hat low on his head, a red kerchief at his neck, worn leather chaps around his slightly bowed legs. It was not the gait she'd seen on Fifty-seventh Street, but it was Colby Sommers.

"Lizzy?" he said as the last of the dust cloud drifted off. "My God, it *is* you."

She stepped out the door, amazed, her heart tripping. "C-Colby," she stammered, "I didn't expect to see you."

"I was up on the bluffs, saw a car coming up the drive and figured I'd better investigate. You're the last person I'd have guessed."

He stopped maybe ten feet from her. The underarms of his faded blue shirt were soaked, his face and neck streaked with muddy rivulets of sweat.

"Lord," he said, looking down at himself, "I'd greet you properly, but I smell like a mule."

She wrung her hands self-consciously. "It's hot. A lot hotter than I remember."

He chuckled and moved cautiously toward her, extending his gloved hands, his grin as wide as Texas. "You look wonderful," he said, taking her hands. "But what in the hell are you doing out here?"

"Sentimental journey," she said self-consciously. "I was in Fredericksburg for the ground-breaking of the recreation hall I donated in Dad's name, so I thought I'd drive on out."

The dog, who'd been circling excitedly, his tail wagging, moved off. Colby let go of her hands and stepped back. "I got an invitation a while back, put it on my calendar as a matter of fact, but decided I wouldn't go." He took off his hat and wiped his sweaty brow with the sleeve of his shirt. "Didn't want any sad reminders, if you want to know the truth."

"And here I am in person," she said apologetically. "The saddest reminder of all."

"Had I known you were comin' down, I might have made an effort."

"Maybe I should have sent a personal invitation," she said.

"You were responsible for the one I got, then?"

"Yes," she replied, lowering her eyes.

"I figured as much."

Liz was suddenly very embarrassed.

"Were you going to call me?" he asked. "Or was this just a private visit to the old homestead?"

"I intended to call you, yes. It seemed the polite thing to do, considering I was this close."

The wind kicked up, blowing the skirt of her silk dress against her legs. A tumbleweed rolled across the yard. Liz pushed her curls back off her face, feeling Colby study her.

"Well, no need to stand out in the sun," he said. "I've got a key to the house. We might as well go in. I'll just tether my horse in the shade first."

Liz waited while Colby took his horse over to a small tree near the bunkhouse, then they began walking toward the house. She felt as unsteady as that first trek she'd made across this same patch of ground over ten years ago.

"So you just happened by?" she asked.

"I rode out this morning to look over my herd, but I

got to thinking about that ground-breaking ceremony...which got me to thinking about you...which
got me to thinking about Virgil's place. One thing led
to another, and I ended up here."

"It was the same with me," she said, happy to share
the coincidence. "I was actually headed for the airport
when the urge struck to see Dad's ranch."

"Nice to know we're thinkin' along the same lines,"
he said meaningfully.

"Too bad the place is so run-down," she said, as a
swirl of dust went past them.

"Yes, it's in a sad state, but the sorry truth is that the
buildings aren't worth much to anyone."

They went around the house and climbed up on the
porch. Colby fished in his pocket for his key ring. Liz
waited, her hands folded in front of her.

"That ring finger is lookin' kind of bare," Colby said
with a nod. "What happened?"

"I broke off my engagement with Grayson," she replied.

"I hope I didn't contribute to the problem."

"You did, but only to the extent of helping to open
my eyes."

Colby unlocked the door and had to give it a hard
push to get it open. "Grayson was nice enough," he
said, "but I could tell you had no business marryin'
him."

"The fact that I went to bed with you was a pretty
strong clue, I suppose."

Colby chuckled. "It was for me, anyway."

He motioned for her to enter and Liz stepped inside.
Sheets covered most of the furniture. Colby strode over

to the sofa and chairs, his boots heavy on the creaky old floorboards, and pulled off the sheets.

"I leased it furnished," he said, "so most of Virgil's stuff is still here."

Liz recognized the sofa and chairs. She gazed around the room, memories flooding her mind. The house seemed smaller, of course. Everything did. She could feel her father's presence. The chair her mother had sat in the day she'd come for her drew Liz's attention. She felt a pang of painful remembrance.

"Sit down and make yourself at home," Colby said. "If that old hand pump in the kitchen still works, I'm going to draw some water and wash up a bit."

"You don't have to for my sake, Colby."

"Then I will for mine, sweetheart."

He went off to the kitchen and Liz sat in her mother's chair. She ran her fingers over the worn arms, imagining the horror Margaret must have felt at coming here to take her married daughter home—to save her from a life of physical hardship, of ponytails and suntanned skin, jeans and chicken fried steaks.

Liz heard the rusty creak of the pump. On a couple of occasions when the power was off she'd pumped water by hand to make coffee or wash dishes. "The power goes out in the city, you're through," her father had said. "Here we go to plan B. The name of the game is survival." The remark hadn't meant as much then as it did now. She understood so much more.

Liz got up from the chair and quietly made her way to the kitchen. She felt compelled to intrude on Colby's privacy. He was at the sink, his back to her. He'd stripped off his shirt and was washing his torso with a soapy rag. His dark hair was soaked, the muscles under the tanned skin of his back rippling. The sight of his broad shoulders brought a flood of recollections.

Liz beat a hasty retreat, as much to flee her feelings as Colby. She went to the room that had been hers for those winter months she'd lived with her father. The furniture was unchanged. An old sheet covered the mattress of the single bed. She pulled it off. Off in the distance Colby's dog barked, probably at a jackrabbit. She remembered how Toby used to bark at everything that moved in the night—everything, that is, but her.

Liz sat on the bed. She recalled the hour or so she'd lie there every night, waiting for the sound of her father's snoring to begin before stealing off to make her escape out the back door and into Colby's waiting arms.

She lay on the bed to recapture the feeling. Amazingly even the pattern of cracks in the ceiling looked familiar. Until this moment, she couldn't have said there were any cracks at all, let alone describe the pattern. Everything came flooding back with a rush—the irresistible allure of Colby waiting for her. Of course, back then she'd have walked ten miles barefoot in the snow to be with him.

Closing her eyes, she could remember the feel of his warm skin on her icy body, the steamy moistness of his breath on her neck, his soft lips when he sucked on her turgid nipples. The mere recollection of his touch aroused her.

"Just the way I pictured you," he said from the doorway.

Liz's eyes popped open and she lifted herself to her elbows. "Oh."

Colby was stripped to the waist, his wet hair finger-combed. He still had on his chaps and boots. Her eyes went to the patch of denim showing through the hole in the leather leggings at his groin. A grin crept across his mouth.

"When I'd be in my bunk, waiting for you to come to me, I'd picture you lying here all soft and sweet. Hell of a compelling image."

"I was remembering those days, too," she confessed.

"Were you, Liz?"

She nodded.

"Damned strange the way our minds run along the same track, don't you think?"

She nodded again.

He ambled to the bed and sat down next to her. Liz lay still, her heart starting to pound. He took her hand, playing with her fingers as he stared at them.

"I've thought about you an awful lot the last few months, Lizzy," he said, his voice low like a night wind.

"I've thought a lot about you, too."

"Remember how you used to come to the bunk-house so we could make love?"

"Yes."

"I always thought it was an unequal situation, the rancher's daughter sneakin' off with the help. Me, unable to do a damned thing but hope you'd come."

"I can understand why you'd feel that way."

He touched her ear with his finger, and slowly drew it down her jaw. Then he traced a line on her skin at the neckline of her dress. "I don't imagine you liked the inequality any more than I did."

She shook her head. "I didn't."

Colby looked deep into her eyes. Her body tensed with anticipation. He ran his tongue along the edge of his chapped lip. "Seems to me we have a chance to rectify the inequity."

She looked at him questioningly.

"There's nothing to keep me from your bed now... unless it'd be you."

"I don't want to keep you from my bed," she whispered.

Colby took her jaw in his hand and kissed her mouth as she sank her fingers into his thick, damp hair. Hunger for him ran through her like a fire.

He stood and removed his chaps, unfastening the ties at the back of the legs first, then the heavy buckle in front. The chaps landed in the corner with a thud. Next he took off his boots. Liz got up and began unfastening the tiny buttons running down the front of her dress. As she slipped it off, he embraced her, taking her in his arms so firmly that he lifted her off the floor. Only her toes touched the boards.

They were kissing deeply now, with a ravenous passion. Everything seemed to melt away, and all that was left was the two of them. It could have been his room at the Clairbourne, that cottage at the bed-and-breakfast in Connecticut, the bunkhouse, their dank room at the old residence hotel in New Orleans. They were together, that's all she knew.

Within moments they were naked on the bed. He crushed her small body against his. She gingerly sank her teeth into his shoulder. His skin tasted of soap and sage, his lips tinged with the flavor of her perfume.

"Lizzy, darlin'," he said through gritted teeth. "Lizzy, darlin'." Over and over.

Her insides were in turmoil, her body roiling with desire. She was licking and biting and sucking his flesh, getting all of him she could, giving to him what he would take, permitting him to do whatever he wanted.

When he moved between her legs, she wrapped them around his waist. She was so wet, his shaft slipped easily inside her. Liz drove her heels into his buttocks and dug her nails into his shoulders.

"Oh, Colby," she cried.

He managed to be forceful without hurting her, driving deep inside her so there was no doubt she'd been taken. Claimed. Possessed.

They came together, their bodies an undulating mass, the groans of ecstasy rising from his throat with a greater urgency than she'd ever heard. At last he collapsed on her, his vigor drained. She locked her heels behind him, and gave him a close hug.

Their chests were slick with perspiration, the hair at her temples as wet as his. Only his breathing told her he hadn't died in the act of love. Otherwise, there was little life in him.

"Sweetheart," he said between heavy breaths, "you sure do know how to make love."

"I wasn't sure you still could after what you pulled at that bed-and-breakfast in Connecticut." She gave him a sharp kick in the buttocks with her heel. "That's for being a bastard that night."

He lifted his head and smiled into her eyes. "You came all the way to Texas to tell me I'm a bastard?"

She took his face in his hands, then kissed his lower lip. "That, and to try to figure out why I can't get you out of my system."

"I think we just figured that out, didn't we, sugar?"

She gave him a forlorn look. "It's a pleasant reason I admit, but a damned lousy one."

"What are you sayin'?"

"I feel ashamed of being so weak."

"So what do you want me to do—walk you to your car and send you on your way until the next time?"

"I don't know what I want," she said with a sigh. "Never have and probably never will."

Colby moved off of her, dropping heavily onto the mattress beside her. Liz entwined her fingers in his. Again she stared at the cracks in the ceiling, wondering as she had a decade ago when she'd be with him again.

Colby was silent for a long time. Then he roused himself, rolling to his side and propping himself on his elbow. "I just had an idea," he said.

"What idea?"

"How'd you like to go to New Orleans?"

"What?"

"I said, how'd you like to go to New Orleans?"

"Colby, are you crazy?"

"No, I'm dead serious."

"How we going to get there? On horseback?"

"No, I thought we could take my plane."

"You have an airplane?"

"A little one. But it's got two engines."

"You actually have a plane."

"I figured it was easier than trying to sprout wings and fly."

Liz shook her head. "Colby, you're insane. I can't go to New Orleans. I've got to get back to New York."

He wagged his finger at her. "I won't ask you but once, Lizzy, so think carefully before you say no."

She sighed with resignation, though she still hadn't

decided if she'd go or not. "I guess it's not your fault I'm so easily tempted. Is it because you're irresistible or because I have no resistance?"

"Maybe it's a little bit of both."

"I can't be the only woman who throws herself at you."

"You're the only one who matters."

She stroked his face with her hand, feeling a well of emotion. "You really want to take me to New Orleans?"

"Yep."

"It'd be easier and smarter to say no right now, to nip it in the bud."

He slapped her on the butt. "Quit thinkin', Lizzy, and get dressed. If we hurry, we can make it to Galatoire's for dinner." He was up and putting his clothes on. "I'll have to ride with you back to my place to save time. One of my boys can come over and get my horse later." He picked up her underthings and handed them to her. "Come on, get a move on. You've had a roll in the hay with the Colby Sommers you've always known and loved. Now I'm going to give you a peek at the other Colby Sommers."

He picked up his chaps and folded them over his arm.

"If he makes love like you do, I'm a dead woman."

He gave a laugh. "Sweetheart, I promise you, the fun has just begun."

13

HE WASN'T EXAGGERATING. Colby's ranch was a sophisticated operation. The brick house stood on a rise, surrounded by giant shade trees. The airstrip was off a quarter of a mile in one direction, the outbuildings a quarter of a mile in the other.

"You couldn't have built this in the past few months," she said, marveling as they came up the sweeping drive.

"No, I built the house three years ago."

She looked at him with surprise. "I had no idea you were this successful."

"Never did strike me as very genteel to brag. Anyway, I'm me, Liz, not my money."

"So the oil money isn't responsible for any of this," she said as they came to a stop in front of the house.

"I invested most of that in real estate. Figured it was time I diversify."

His dog, who he'd admitted with embarrassment had been impulsively named Maggie as a backhanded tribute to her mother, whined in the back seat. Colby reached back and opened the door to let her out.

Liz shook her head. "Colby, you're amazing."

"I'm like any other guy, sweetheart. I like to be appreciated for myself, not what I've got in the bank. Your daddy was that way."

"I know, but..."

"But what?"

"You didn't need to hide it. Money's not the issue with us," she said.

"Maybe not money per se, but the way a person lives, the things that matter in his life, are important. The material dimension is only one of several, I grant you, but..."

Now it was her turn. "But what?" she said.

"But if you have nothing, it can limit your options."

"Colby, I never rejected you because you were poor. That wasn't why I let my mother arrange the annulment. Nor does the fact that you have money now make you any more worthy as a human being. Back at Dad's place I made love with Colby Sommers, the person, not Colby Sommers the tycoon."

"I don't mean to bring up a sore subject, sugar," he said drolly, "but it's Colby Sommers the person you've sent packin' every time we've been together."

Liz fell silent.

"I didn't mean that as a criticism," he said.

"No, I understand your point. And it probably shows why this is not a very good idea."

Colby slipped his hand under her hair, caressing the nape of her neck. "I wish I could figure out what you're afraid of. It's baffled me all the years I've known you."

Liz bowed her head. "I'm afraid of my feelings for you. I have been from the day we met."

He lifted her chin, turning her face toward him. "Forget fear and don't worry about your feelings," he said. "What we both need is less thinking and more enjoying. Come on, I bet you'd like to clean up and change before we head for the Big Easy."

They went inside. Colby introduced her to his

housekeeper, Emma, a petite woman of sixty. Emma had an engaging manner and a sparkle in her eye. Taking Liz's case, she led the way to the guest suite so Liz could get cleaned up while Colby took care of business that needed his attention.

The house, Liz noted, was nicely decorated. Considering Colby's affluence, it was no surprise that it was furnished expensively. But tastefully—that wasn't a given. She asked Emma if he'd had some professional help.

"Yes, ma'am. He brought in a fancy decorator from Dallas to help, though Mr. Sommers picked out many of the antiques himself. Seems he can't go to New Orleans without buyin' somethin' for the house. Mrs. Johnston, the decorator, told me he has a good eye. His weakness, she said, was color, but that's true of most men—according to her, anyway."

"So Colby goes to New Orleans a lot."

"New Orleans and New York especially. Been to London several times, too. He likes the theater a whole lot, that's mainly why. Always seemed strange to me, considerin' his roots. Folks around here call him the "gentleman rancher," cause of his fancy taste in things, and his love of travel. But he's a right sharp businessman, too. Folks respect him. There ain't many men in west Texas that started out with so little and come as far as he has in so short a time."

They entered the guest suite. It was cheerfully decorated with a combination of old and new pieces, the colors beige and peach. "Colby's more complex than he seems on the surface," Liz said.

"Yes, ma'am."

"He's still a man of the land, but he has this other side, too," Liz observed.

"That's Mr. Sommers, all right."

"Amazing how a person's prejudices can blind them," Liz said, feeling an unexpected well of excitement at seeing this other side of Colby.

"Ma'am?"

"I realize I'm only just now getting to know the real Colby Sommers."

"Beggin' your pardon, Miss Cabot," Emma said, "but you're the young lady who was once married to Mr. Sommers, if I'm not mistaken."

"That's right."

The woman nodded thoughtfully.

"Has Colby mentioned me?"

"We've never had a proper conversation about you, but I recall hearin' the name. Not surprised you're so pretty and all. Would have been surprised if you wasn't, if you want to know the truth."

"Thank you."

"It's a plain fact."

"I would imagine Colby gets the attention of a number of attractive women."

Emma smiled ruefully. "If so, ma'am, you won't be hearin' it from me." She headed for the door. "Anything you be wantin', Miss Cabot, just give a holler."

"All I need is a shower and to change my clothes."

The housekeeper paused at the door. "Mr. Sommers could be tied up talkin' to his bookkeeper for a spell, but I reckon he'll be ready soon. Has to if you're goin' to be havin' supper in New Orleans. It'll be a late supper in any case, that's for sure."

The woman left and Liz went to the window that

overlooked a flower garden. A man was at the far side, pulling weeds. During the drive in, she'd seen a couple of cowboys working the cattle. He'd told her at times his payroll ran to a dozen or more, including office staff and domestic help. She'd said she had no idea it took so many people to run a ranch. Colby said his bookkeeper and secretary looked after a lot more than just ranch business and that cowboying was seasonal work.

Liz went off to shower, feeling a delight she'd never known before—not in connection with Colby Sommers, anyway. Passion, lustfulness she'd experienced with him, anxiety and sorrow, too, but this was a first time for delight. It was both humbling and exciting. And it felt damned good.

IT WAS ALREADY DARK as the Cessna glided onto the runway at Moisant Field in New Orleans. Colby had told her that although he had been instrument-rated for a year, he preferred not to make night landings with passengers. "It's one thing to take your own life into your hands, another altogether to take someone else's. Had there been time, I'd have arranged for a professional pilot to accompany us," he'd said.

Liz had appreciated the responsibility he'd shown, but if there was any chance of danger, she was perfectly willing to share it. Besides, Colby seemed entirely competent and very much in control.

She'd had very different feelings about him as a person and as a man, almost from the moment she'd walked into his house that afternoon. A whole new world had opened up. Which was not to say that the man on horseback that afternoon wasn't real. To the contrary, he was the man she'd always loved, with a deep passion. But this other Colby, the one who'd flown her to New Orleans, seemed more of her world.

It wasn't as though she'd never seen this side of him before. He'd spoken of coming to New York regularly, of enjoying theater and good restaurants. She'd seen him in a sport coat and sweater the day they'd driven up to Connecticut. She'd known he had other dimensions, but she hadn't let herself accept them. She'd been too busy trying to convince herself that it was Grayson Bartholomew who fitted into the kind of life she wanted.

As soon as Colby had come for her in his living room, showered and wearing a crisp white dress shirt and steel gray slacks, a blazer over his arm, she'd told herself to relax and go with the flow. She was determined to experience Colby as he was. That had probably been what Moira had been trying to tell her when they'd talked at the wedding reception.

And so, flying across Texas with the sun setting behind them, Liz got to know the man she'd been denying. Yes, Colby was still that cowboy in chaps. Yes, he loved the ranching life. "There's no therapy like having a horse under you and the open sky above your head," he'd said. But they talked about theater, about New York, about adventures into different worlds.

Liz could see there was a lot Colby could teach her about Broadway and off Broadway, about antiques, not to mention Texas barbecue and branding. And there was a lot she could teach him about music, especially classical music. Nor was Colby a skier, a shortcoming she told him he definitely had to rectify. "If you're in New York during the winter, and have extra time, I'll take you to Vermont and teach you to ski," she said.

Colby, who'd had his headset back off one ear during the flight so he could listen to her and monitor the radio at the same time, put his hand on her knee. "Sweetheart," he said, "I plan on being in New York a whole lot. And I guarantee you won't have any trouble encitin' me to come on a skiing weekend in Vermont. The part where you sit around by the fire at night, I've already got down pat."

"Yeah," she said, "it's getting you away from the fire and into bed, that's the hard part."

He'd cuffed her chin. "You're never going to let me forget that, are you, Lizzy?"

"I could have killed you, just killed you."

"Why? Because you were embarrassed, or because you wanted me so much, you couldn't stand it?"

She gave him a jab with her elbow. "That arrogance of yours is something else we have to work on."

Once Colby's Cessna was parked in the tie-down area, they deplaned. A limousine was waiting for them outside the hangar. "I phoned from the ranch," he explained as they climbed in the back. "The folks at Galatoire's have been alerted that we're on the way. If necessary, they'll keep the cook there until our arrival."

Colby sat in the corner and Liz nestled against him, seeing no point in being coy. "What's so special about Galatoire's that you're going to all this trouble?" she asked.

"The redfish, topped with crab, is to die for," he said. "My favorite waiter, an old fellow who's been there for fifty years, told me the dish is a damned good aphrodisiac," he said with a wink.

"Oh, I see. Who do you think needs it—you or me?"

Colby kissed her on the mouth. "Let's just say it's for our mutual pleasure."

There were only a few diners left when they arrived, but the bearded maitre d' greeted them warmly and took them to a table in the far back corner. The decor wasn't fancy. The side walls were mirrored, rows of fans hung from the ceiling. The place had an old-world feel, a condition amplified by the fact that the waiters were in tuxedos.

Colby's favorite waiter, an old fellow named Ernie, greeted them with a warmth that was sufficiently understated to seem sincere. "Redfish tonight, Mr. Sommers?" he said.

"Please, Ernie. And a bottle of that Fetzer chardonnay."

"Care to start with a little gumbo?"

"Please."

The man went off, moving with a deliberateness that belied his efficiency. Colby took her hands.

"Not quite like the last time we were in this town, huh, sweetheart?"

"We dreamed about dinner in a place like this, didn't we?"

"And we've finally made it. Took a while, but here we are."

"Ironic, isn't it?" she said.

"Personally, I think it was destined."

"Do you believe in destiny, Colby?"

He brushed her cheek with the back of his fingers. "How can I not?"

THE LIMO DROPPED THEM off in the brick courtyard of the Windsor Court Hotel under the protective gaze of a huge bronze knight in full armor. The lobby of the hotel was sumptuous. On the antique table in the middle was an enormous arrangement of long-stem pink roses. Liz could see Colby had decided to spare no expense.

But it wasn't until they were shown into the penthouse suite that she fully realized to what lengths he'd gone. The sitting room, adorned by a grand piano, Chinese screens and quality works of art, would have made Donald Trump proud. The centerpiece of the bedroom was a huge canopied bed. Colby tipped the bellhop, then joined her. Liz turned to him as he entered the room.

"You want to make up, in one night, for all those weeks we spent in that fleabag hotel, don't you?"

"I want New Orleans to have better connotations," he said.

Liz took his hands. "The memories of those days are among the most precious I have," she said, her eyes shimmering. "They were tough, but I was with the man I loved."

"Or so you thought at the time."

"Yes, but that doesn't detract from what we shared."

Colby nodded. "I know. I feel the same."

She pulled his face down and kissed his lips. "Thank you for this," she whispered. "Thank you for caring."

"Can I tell you a little secret?" he said.

"What?"

"After we closed the Continental American deal, and I got my check, I flew down here to celebrate. Stayed here, at the Windsor Court, right here in the penthouse suite."

"Alone?"

"Yes, alone. It was one of the most miserable nights of my life. Something terribly important was missing. I didn't want to admit it, but I knew it was you."

She touched his cheek. "And I was too stupid to realize this is where I should have been."

Colby peered deep into her eyes. "Have we passed some sort of milestone, or is it just my imagination?"

"I don't want to think about that now," she said. "I just want to enjoy being with you."

He kissed her deeply, very deeply, then scooped her up and carried her to the bed. "You're still just a mite, aren't you?"

"Big enough to take care of you, cowboy."

He gently laid her on the bed, then sat next to her. He pushed her blond curls back off her face. "I love you, Lizzy," he said, his eyes shimmering, "just like I did ten years ago and, I guess, just as I have ever since."

He kissed her softly on the lips.

"I must love you, too," she said.

"What makes you say that?"

"I don't mind the fact that you call me Lizzy anymore. In fact, I like it."

He laughed. "Old habits die hard."

"Yeah, I know. Seems I never did get you out of my heart."

He put his hand on her breast. She could feel the warmth of his palm right through the fabric of her dress. Liz knew she'd never be able to get enough of this man. He was the love of her life. And when he began slowly undressing her, she felt the fever again—the fever of desire that only Colby Sommers could create.

14

WHILE LIZ SHOWERED the next morning, Colby ordered breakfast from room service so that it would be waiting when she came out of the bath. He wanted everything to be perfect for her, so he'd ordered all her favorites: fresh-squeezed orange juice, omelettes and coffee.

He sighed. Wonderful as the nights were with Liz, there was something about seeing her shining face first thing in the morning that was food for his soul. That had been his main joy during the few short months of their marriage—awakening with her in his bed.

After breakfast, they roamed the French Quarter, mostly haunting the antique shops on Royal Street. They had done that as newlyweds a decade earlier. Liz, as he recalled, had a special fondness for antique jewelry. Now, of course, she wasn't so shy about trying on some of the fine old estate pieces. She told him workmanship like that just wasn't done anymore.

Colby took pleasure in seeing her trying on rings and bracelets and earrings. He watched her face carefully to gauge her delight, having decided he wanted to get her something as a remembrance of their trip. Several times he offered to buy her a piece she seemed to particularly admire, but she always declined, saying it was much too expensive or not quite right.

As the day passed, as they walked arm in arm in the French Quarter, he found himself feeling increasingly more comfortable with her. Liz was so much more than another woman he found attractive. Her company just plain felt good. He hadn't recalled feeling that at ease with her, even when she was his wife.

Liz, too, seemed more relaxed. She was enjoying herself a lot, he could tell. Though they'd come to a tacit understanding that they wouldn't worry about tomorrow, Colby sensed that she was testing her feelings for him, wondering if there was a way this might continue.

The thought had crossed his mind more than once, as well. In fact, everything that happened—every look, every glance, every smile—asked if it had to end here, or if there was a way they could continue to be together.

In one of his favorite antique stores Colby found an eighteenth-century French farm table in fruitwood that he had to have for his study. He told Liz he'd use it as a library table, maybe even put his computer on it. In a fit of tit for tat, she offered to buy it for him, though the price was several thousand dollars. "I can't let you," he said, "unless, of course, you let me buy you one of those rings or bracelets you saw today." Liz told him he was a tyrant, but was mollified when he allowed her to buy him a chinoiserie box to put on his new table.

They decided it was time to head back to the hotel and, as they walked along the street, Liz asked him if they could go by the residential hotel they'd lived in a decade ago. Colby told her it was gone. "I went to see it my first few trips back," he said, "but three years ago when I was here, I discovered it'd been torn down and an office building had gone up in its place."

"Too bad. I'd have liked to have seen it."

"I don't know about you," he said, putting an arm

around her shoulder, "but I recall the weeks we spent there as vividly as any experience of my life."

Liz agreed.

It was around four when they got back to the hotel. Colby suggested they have high tea, telling her, "It's the best you'll ever have outside England."

And so they had tea in front of a carved marble fireplace as a woman nearby plucked the strings of a harp, the music soft, relaxing, genteel. It was the sort of experience he'd have never been able to give her a decade earlier, and he was pleased to be able to afford it now. And in truth, he didn't think they'd have enjoyed it this much ten years ago. There was an advantage to being older, wiser and more sophisticated.

In fact, it struck him that their relative maturity might make a lot of things possible that weren't workable a decade earlier. He took her hand as they listened to the harp music and had their scones and tea.

For a long time they looked into each other's eyes, not saying a word. It was then that it came into his mind exactly what he had to do. The clarity of it was almost astounding.

He looked at his watch. "Lizzy, there's some business I need to take care of, so I'm going to let you go on up to the suite alone, if you don't mind."

"Business?"

"Something I have to take care of right away. I won't be too long. I should be back in half an hour or so."

"Take as long as you like. I can use the opportunity to have a nice relaxing bath and dress for dinner."

Colby took care of the bill and they went to the lobby where he gave her a kiss and then left, heading at a brisk walk back to the French Quarter.

LIZ LAY SOAKING in the tub, thinking about their day. It was idyllic. That was what scared her. Where could things go from there? That was the question they'd been facing from the very first day they'd met.

So maybe their worlds weren't quite so different as she'd first thought, but they still didn't exactly live around the corner from each other. They might be able to come together in spirit, but the same couldn't be said of their homes, their work, their friends, their lives. Did that mean they could only be together when time and circumstance allowed?

These were practical questions that needed to be faced, but Liz didn't want to face them. Not yet. And so she would go on dreaming this dream with Colby, running from practicalities, the way they used to run from the harsh reality of life by climbing on the St. Charles Avenue trolley and riding it to the end of the line. That was life. There was always an end of the line.

What to do about that was the question everybody faced. Enjoy it while you can, was probably as good an answer as any. She could almost hear Colby saying something like that. "Come on, Lizzy, don't let tomorrow spoil today."

After she'd soaked enough, Liz climbed from the tub and dressed. A few minutes after she'd gone into the salon to wait for him, Colby rushed in. "Sorry," he said, on seeing she was already dressed. "It'll only take me a sec."

He gave her a quick kiss and went off. Minutes later he was back, dressed in a navy suit. He looked awfully handsome and she told him so.

"Can I ask you a silly question?" she said.

"Sure."

"Why is it that when you're in a suit your legs aren't bowed?"

He laughed and kissed her on the cheek. "Sweetheart, they would be if I'd spent the last couple of hours on a horse."

They left the hotel and headed west, instead of north toward the French Quarter. Liz asked where they were going.

"It's a nice evening," he said. "I have a little treat in mind."

A few blocks from the Windsor Court they came to St. Charles Avenue. When she saw the trolley tracks, she got excited. They waited at the stop and, when a trolley came along a few minutes later, they climbed aboard. Liz felt absolutely gleeful.

"What a wonderful idea," she said as they settled into their favorite seat in front where they could see the tracks ahead and the leafy canopy formed by the shade trees along the avenue.

Liz sat on the edge of her seat, watching the familiar streets of New Orleans roll by, the sweet, humid air wafting through the open windows, the clang of the trolley bell a sort of one-note jazz filled with bittersweet memories.

They got off the trolley at Audubon Park and strolled in the evening air. They even managed to find the bench where they had sat to discuss their return to Texas. Liz wanted to sit on it again.

"I remember the day so well," she said as a tingly feeling went through her.

"Yes," he said, "it was painful."

She studied his face, seeing the nostalgia, but this was not the same Colby Sommers. He'd been brave, even as a young man, but there was a confidence and a serenity about him now that hadn't been there before. She realized that he was a man at peace with himself, and that was terribly, terribly compelling.

They rode in the trolley all the way back to the French Quarter, walking through the crowded streets to the restaurant Colby had chosen for dinner, the Court of Two Sisters. They dined in an open courtyard under a huge shade tree and a canopy of vines, serenaded by a jazz trio playing softly nearby. The air was so clear and fragrant, and Colby seemed so happy and content, Liz couldn't help feeling happy, too—as happy, perhaps, as she'd ever been in her life.

They ate gumbo and boiled shrimp and ribs and salad until they didn't have room for another bite. But then Colby went back to the buffet and brought them each bowls of homemade vanilla ice cream with praline sauce. Liz nearly killed herself, but she ate every bite.

"This has been a wonderful meal, a wonderful day, a wonderful trip," she told him. "I'll never forget it."

"I agree, sugar. If there's a downside, it's that I don't want it to end."

"Neither do I."

He looked deeply into her eyes, the love she saw stronger than ever. "Lizzy, while we were having tea this afternoon, a thought occurred to me."

"What's that?"

"I think we deserve many tomorrows together, as many as the good Lord will give us. What I'm tryin' to say is that in this day and age a lady lawyer from New York and a free-spirited cowboy from Texas ought to be able to find a way to be together, if the will is there."

He reached across the table and took her hand. "You see, Lizzy, I love you. Always have, always will."

Her eyes teared up immediately. "And I love you, Colby. I want to be with you every bit as much as you want to be with me, but how realistic is it?"

"The question is how flexible can you be? I have no problem splittin' time between New York and the ranch. And maybe there's a way you can make your practice relevant in Texas as well as New York. Being an oil tycoon yourself, you have to have picked up some knowledge of the business."

She was incredibly touched. "I have to admit the thought has crossed my mind."

"Well, I don't want you gettin' upset," he said, reaching into his pocket, "but there was a ring I saw you eyein' when we were browsing this afternoon. I'd like for you to have it."

He opened his hand. In his palm was the three carat, heart-shaped antique diamond ring she'd drooled over. Her mouth sagged open.

"Oh, Colby," she said, afraid to touch it.

He took the ring and slipped it on her finger. "I like the shape of it," he said. "Reminds me of a very special day in our lives."

"It's beautiful," she said, tears running down her cheeks.

"This is comin' fast I know," he said, "and we have plenty of time to plan and figure out a way to make it work, but...well, if you could see your way, come next Valentine's Day, I think we ought to get married again."

"Colby..." she said, weeping softly.

"That'll give us plenty of time to work things out,

and the very worst that could happen is you'll have this ring to remember the good days we've had in the past.''

She was speechless. Colby went around the table, helped her to her feet and held her in his arms. There were a hundred eyes looking her way, but Liz didn't care. She was in the arms of the man she loved.

_____Epilogue_____

February 14

"GIRL," ARIEL SAID, "how you going to know what to think every time February 14 comes around? This has got to be the most confusing day of the year—Valentine's Day, birthday, two marriages. If you have a baby on this day a year or two from now, it's going to be all over."

Everybody laughed, but nobody harder than Liz. She was nervous, the same way she'd been the last time she married. But having all her friends with her while she dressed made it easier.

"The hell with Liz," Wendy said dryly. "Think of poor Colby—his annual gift budget down the tubes in one day!"

Moira, her pregnant stomach only starting to show under her pale pink bridesmaid's dress, stepped next to Liz and put her arm around her. "You're a gorgeous bride," she said, "and I _love_ the dress."

"You don't think a red wedding dress on Valentine's Day is too cheeky, even for me?"

"I think it's perfect."

Angela and Pam were standing to the side, admiring Liz's dress in her mother's full-length mirror. "Two thumbs-up," Angela said, approvingly.

Pam was smiling, though not so broadly as the evening she showed up at the Thursday Night Club with the ring Grayson had given her. Their wedding was planned for June. "I'll be taking notes."

"Liz Cabot has the most unorthodox style in the world when it comes to engagements, weddings, Valentine's Day and men," Wendy had said. "God knows what she'll come up with next."

Liz had taken her friends' ribbing in good spirits, even when they'd pointed out that she had the distinction of being the only member who'd gotten kicked out of the Thursday Night Club twice. "Well, I finally got it right," she'd said in reply.

Ariel was at the window, noting that it was snowing again. "I hope we can get to the church."

"I have a feeling Colby would make sure Liz got there," Moira said, "even if he had to come for her on horseback."

"Though a dogsled might be more appropriate," Wendy intoned.

The bedroom door opened and Margaret Cabot entered, her face shining with happiness. In her hands were long-stem red roses. She proceeded to hand one to each of the women. "These are from Colby," she said. "He wanted me to give one to each of his favorite city girls."

"How romantic," somebody gushed.

"Yeah, where can I find *me* a cowboy?" Ariel said.

Margaret had two roses left. She handed one to Liz. "One for you, darling, and the dear boy had one for me, as well."

They embraced.

"I take it this time you approve," Liz said, her eyes glossy.

"How can a woman not want a son-in-law who named his beloved dog after her?"

"His dog?" Wendy said.

"I'm assuming in Texas it's a compliment," Margaret said. "If not...well, if not, I guess I just have to lump it, don't I?"

They all laughed, gathering around Liz. She looked at each of them in turn, her friends and her mother. "This is the happiest day, the best Valentine's Day, the most wonderful birthday of my life," she said. "I'm so glad you're here to share it with me."

"This ain't nothin'," Ariel said. "Wait until tonight."

Liz blushed and everybody cheered.

"This day never would have happened if I hadn't had a change of heart about my life, what I needed and wanted," Liz told them. "It all started a year ago today, so in a way, you're all partly responsible. The Thursday Night Club gave me the courage to live my fantasies and follow my heart." She kissed her mother on the cheek. "And if you hadn't made me get that annulment, I wouldn't be getting married today."

Margaret smiled ruefully. "Sometimes Mother knows best."

"You know," Liz said, "I think the biggest stumbling block was your marriage to Dad. When I saw the two of you together I knew it had been a mistake, that oil and water just didn't mix. For the longest time I was sure the same was true of Colby and me."

"There are times," her mother said, "when a man and a woman love each other so much they find a way to make a life, no matter what. It isn't easy. It takes work and a whole lot of love."

"I'd walk to Texas, if I had to be with him," Liz said. "And he'd walk here to be with me."

"What more could a woman want?" Moira said.

They all chimed in together. "Especially on Valentine's Day!"

"Well, girls," Margaret said, "I hate to sound like the mother hen, but it *is* time to head for the church."

LIZ WAS SO HAPPY, her nervousness seemed like a gift. Thankfully, good old stolid Weldon was like a rock. As they stood outside the doors of the sanctuary waiting for the first chords of the music to sound, he kept patting her hand and mumbling she was a beautiful bride and Colby was a very fortunate man. Moira, who was standing just in front of them, turned and gave Liz a cheery smile. She said nothing. It wasn't necessary.

The music sounded, the doors opened and Moira stepped forward. Then she started down the aisle. Liz clung to Weldon's arm.

When the lull in the music came, they moved forward to the arch of the doorway and the sanctuary opened before them. She was aware of the expectant, smiling faces of friends and family looking her way. She could smell the red roses that festooned the hall. On the altar, there were huge bouquets, and garlands, looped in the shape of floral hearts. The church was festive, joyful. It was vivid yet dreamlike; Liz wouldn't have been surprised to see fanciful cupids hovering in the vaulted heights of the nave.

As the first chords of the "Wedding March" sounded, Weldon said, "Here we go, my dear."

They took their first step toward the altar. It was then she saw Colby, in his tuxedo, move to the opening at the end of the aisle so that he could see her. His red bow tie was as joyful as her dress. He looked so handsome.

But then her eyes began to shimmer, glossing so that she could scarcely see his face. She blinked away her tears, sobs and giddy laughter welling within her. It was all she could do to keep from running down the aisle and throwing herself into his arms, but she held herself in check.

The long walk—the walk that had begun on that snowy stretch of ground between her father's home in Texas and the bunkhouse where Colby had slept—had come to an end at last. She left Weldon's arm for Colby Sommers's. Her husband-to-be gave her a smile that said he was the happiest man alive.

The cloud that had hung over their first nuptials was no more. She was with her man. Together again, and at last. On this Valentine's Day and for all the rest to come.

* * *

IT HAPPENED ONE NIGHT
continues with After the Loving
by Sandy Steen.
Available in March 1998
only in Temptation®.

Spoil yourself next month
with these four novels from

Temptation®

THE BLACK SHEEP by Carolyn Andrews

Nick Heagerty was a loner, a rebel *with* a cause. Ten years ago
he'd been accused of a crime he didn't commit—and he'd left
town without a backward glance. Now he was back—but not for
long. Then *everything* changed when he met gorgeous P.I. Andie
Field and realized that his wandering days were numbered...

WISHES by Rita Clay Estrada

When Virginia Gallagher found a wallet full of cash, it would've
been the answer to her prayers, *if* she hadn't been so honest.
When Wilder Hunnicut came to pick it up, *he* would've been a
wish come true, *if* he hadn't been out of her league. And when
her reward was a lamp with three wishes, she started hoping
wishes really could come true...

AFTER THE LOVING by Sandy Steen

It Happened One Night

To claim her inheritance, Isabella Farentino must find a
husband—fast! The only man around is the arrogant,
infuriatingly sexy Cade McBride. Belle's counting on his love-
and-leave-them attitude to get him out of her life, but after one
incredible wedding night with Cade, she's having second
thoughts...

BRIDE OVERBOARD by Heather MacAllister

Brides on the Run

Blair Thomason was about to take the plunge—into marriage,
that is. But when she found herself on a yacht, about to marry a
crook, she plunged into the sea instead! Luckily, Drake O'Keefe
was there to rescue her... She'd barely escaped marrying one
man, only to be stranded with another!

PARTY TIME!

How would you like to win a year's supply of Mills & Boon® Books? Well, you can and they're FREE! Simply complete the competition below and send it to us by 31st August 1998. The first five correct entries picked after the closing date will each win a year's subscription to the Mills & Boon series of their choice. What could be easier?

BALLOONS	BUFFET	ENTERTAIN
STREAMER	DANCING	INVITE
DRINKS	CELEBRATE	FANCY DRESS
MUSIC	PARTIES	HANGOVER

S	O	E	T	A	R	B	E	L	E	C
T	E	F	M	U	S	I	C	D	D	H
S	U	I	V	Z	T	E	Y	R	A	A
N	E	N	T	E	R	T	A	I	N	N
O	B	V	E	R	E	H	K	N	C	G
O	J	I	F	O	A	L	R	K	I	O
L	M	T	F	V	M	P	U	S	N	V
L	P	E	U	Q	E	N	Z	S	G	E
A	W	G	B	X	R	C	T	B	Y	R
B	F	A	N	C	Y	D	R	E	S	S

C8B

Please turn over for details of how to enter...

HOW TO ENTER

Can you find our twelve party words? They're all hidden somewhere in the grid. They can be read backwards, forwards, up, down or diagonally. As you find each word in the grid put a line through it. When you have completed your wordsearch, don't forget to fill in the coupon below, pop this page into an envelope and post it today—you don't even need a stamp!

Mills & Boon Party Time! Competition
FREEPOST CN81, Croydon, Surrey, CR9 3WZ
EIRE readers send competition to PO Box 4546, Dublin 24.

Please tick the series you would like to receive if you are one of the lucky winners

Presents™ ❏ Enchanted™ ❏ Medical Romance™ ❏
Historical Romance™ ❏ Temptation® ❏

Are you a Reader Service™ Subscriber?   Yes ❏   No ❏

Mrs/Ms/Miss/Mr ....Intials ....
(BLOCK CAPITALS PLEASE)

Surname...

Address ....

....

....Postcode...........................

(I am over 18 years of age)   C8B

One application per household. Competition open to residents of the UK and Ireland only. You may be mailed with offers from other reputable companies as a result of this application. If you would prefer not to receive such offers, please tick box. ❏

Closing date for entries is 31st August 1998.

Mills & Boon® is a registered trademark of Harlequin Mills & Boon Limited.

JANICE
KAISER

FAIR
GAME

Dana Kirk is a rich and successful woman, but someone
wants to kill her and her teenage daughter. Who hates
her enough to terrorise this single mother? Detective
Mitchell Cross knows she needs help—
his help—to stay alive.

*"...enough plot twists and turns to delight
armchair sleuths"* —Publishers Weekly

1-55166-065-2
AVAILABLE FROM MARCH 1998

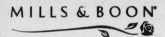

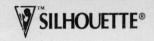

SPECIAL OFFER £5 OFF

FLYING FLOWERS

Beautiful fresh flowers, sent by 1st class post to any UK and Eire address.

We have teamed up with Flying Flowers, the UK's premier 'flowers by post' company, to offer you £5 off a choice of their two most popular bouquets the 18 mix (CAS) of 10 multihead and 8 luxury bloom Carnations and the 25 mix (CFG) of 15 luxury bloom Carnations, 10 Freesias and Gypsophila. All bouquets contain fresh flowers 'in bud', added greenery, bouquet wrap, flower food care instructions, and personal message card. They are boxed, gift wrapped and sen by 1st class post.

To redeem £5 off a Flying Flowers bouquet simply complete the application form below and send it with your cheque or postal ord to; **HMB Flying Flowers Offer, The Jersey Flower Centre, Jersey JE1 5FI**

ORDER FORM (Block capitals please) Valid for delivery anytime until 30th November 1998 MAB/0198/A

Title .... Initials .... Surname ....

Address..

....Postcode ....

Signature...Are you a Reader Service Subscriber **YES/N**

Bouquet(s) **18 CAS** (Usual Price £14.99) **£9.99** ☐   **25 CFG** (Usual Price £19.99) **£14.99** ☐

I enclose a cheque/postal order payable to Flying Flowers for £....................................or payment

VISA/MASTERCARD ☐☐☐☐☐☐☐☐☐☐☐☐☐☐☐☐ Expiry Date............/............/......

PLEASE SEND MY BOUQUET TO ARRIVE BY........../............/........

TO Title .... Initials .... Surname ....

Address..

....Postcode ....

Message (Max 10 Words) ....

....

Please allow a minimum of four working days between receipt of order and 'required by date' for delive

You may be mailed with offers from other reputable companies as a result of this application. Please tick box if you would prefer not to receive such offers. ☐

Terms and Conditions Although dispatched by 1st class post to arrive by the required date the exact day of delivery cannot be guarantee Valid for delivery anytime until 30th November 1998. Maximum of 5 redemptions per household, photocopies of the voucher will be accepted.